THE WELDON TRILOGY

BOOK ONE
Fate Intertwined

Michael Randolph

PublishAmerica
Baltimore

Hardcover 978-1-4626-2520-8
Softcover 978-1-4626-2521-5
PUBLISHED BY PUBLISHAMERICA, LLLP
www.publishamerica.com
Baltimore

Printed in the United States of America

Dedication

To my wonderful daughter
Brittany
She inspires me everyday
To reach for the heavens

TABLE OF CONTENTS

Prologue

King Roanoled looks out upon his newly won land. Standing beside him to his right is his high councilor Melcore, "The southerners are finally withdrawing My Lord; they refuse to pass beyond the southern edge of the mountains." Looking down beyond the castle walls, the last few Turiec are being buried out in the ice fields. Thinking back on the last few days, King Roanoled ponders on the fate of his people. They will suffer in this harsh land.

A blazing streak of light burns overhead, slowly vanishing into the southern sky.

Melcore looks at his king, tall, with brown hair held back with a simple circlet of gold. The cares of their people weigh heavily on his shoulders. His gold and black armor shines like the first day he donned it. Hanging from his back is wellimer, his long broadsword. Named for the last High King of Mellost, now gone for many generations, even within its finely wrought sheath, Melcore can feel the immense power flowing from the blade.

Over the long years the Weldons have slowly lost territory after territory to the new southern kings. Now, they have been forced to the last remaining land that they could flee to Though, in so doing, the Turiec people have been forced out of their land and cast into the deep north. A death sentence he is sure. Thinking of the horrific battle that had played out, Melcore does not see how even with a leader such as Meroth, that the Turiec people could survive more than a short period of time in that desolate waste.

Abruptly turning around, King Roanoled commands Melcore to follow him. Leading his high councilor into the castle, they follow many twisting paths and hallways deep into the lower castle. Only the King and Melcore know of these deep ways. Many hours of walking bring through dark lonely halls bring them to an open room looking out to the southern country. High up on the side of the mountains, they stand looking out at their land that the Weldons have fled. For minutes they both are lost in thought looking out onto the plains far below. The two men watch small pinpricks of light stream down the mountainside toward great army camped before the forest at the foot of the mountains.

"Melcore our people will not survive this land we now call home. My time in this world has come to an end; you must call the council together and lead them."

"Nay, My Lord, Your time is still long. You assuredly cannot leave us now," pleads Melcore. King Roanoled turns towards a great high arched door leading into a great throne room. "Melcore, this has been the Weldon way throughout time. Each King has always known his time to journey into the mists of time. This time has been chosen for me by our ancestors." King Roanoled, seeing his friend and councilor Melcore weighed down by the responsibility of his peoples plight. Reaching out to Melcore, he lightly touches his shoulder. "Thank you, my friend, lead our people well."

Swiftly turning around King Roanoled makes his way to the throne room door. Stopping before he goes through, he turns looking back to Melcore. Slowly, fading into a ghostly image, the King intones his final words.

"When our people have become lost and desperate in this cold land, a new King shall come. A Weldon born in another land, our people shall be broken, scattered them to the winds. Yet, under him the lands shall unite, becoming once again a nation. For the world will tremble and despair from an enemy to the north. For the High King shall come again in the time of strife and turmoil in the lands of Mellost."

King Roanoled fades into the mists of time never to be seen by his people again. Turning away with his eyes brimming with tears, He looks out at the army gathered below With a slow resolve Melcore whispers to himself. "My lord, I swear by the ancestors this boy will not lead our people back to the southern lands. This day I swear I will perish before I see our people destroyed!"

Chapter One
The boy that is to become a man

"Ranwulf, pay attention to me and stop daydreaming!" scolds Fetiun.

It has been a long hard year in this cold barren land. The days go by tortuously slow. I study until my mind screams for relief. When I am not studying long forgotten books, I am out in the courtyard learning the art of self-defense, losing count of the bruises a long time ago. I see my classmates laughing and having fun.

"Ouch!" I yell when I feel the stick hit me in the shoulder. Fetiun is standing in front of me while the other kids snicker behind their hands. "I have spoken for the last time, if you don't pay attention you will be punished, do you understand?" Fetiun demanded. Looking down at my papers scattered around my desk I dare not look up, "Yes Master Fetiun, I understand," I answer.

Fetiun walks to the front of the class, laying the hated stick on his desk. "Well, I will give all of you a present for the New Year, and you may thank Ranwulf for it!" He intones. The class looks back at me and scowls. "It will not kill you to study more than you do, since everyone will have plenty of time to enjoy the New Year's festival." Fetiun declares. "I expect for everyone to write an essay on why we celebrate the New Year, in essay form, with no less than two thousand words!"

Shrinking back in my chair from the glares of everyone, I fully realize the next few weeks will be harder than normal. "That will be all for the next two weeks, class dismissed," Fetiun says. Quickly gathering my books, I jump out of my chair and make it out of the door before the rest of the class. Running without looking back, I make it to the tower stairs before anyone can see which way I went. Taking the steps two at a time, I make it three stories before I have to slow down. Below me, I hear the kids screaming my name, taunting me.

Going up the last few flights, I make it to my secret hiding place. I know I only have a short time before I have to be in the courtyard for my lesson. Running up to a blank part of the wall, I press a block in the center, with a grinding noise a small part of it moves inward. I hear voices coming up behind me from the stairs. "Ranwulf, where are you, we just want to talk!" one of the kids yells. Thinking to myself, 'I am not dumb as a fellar.' Quickly squeezing inside my hole, I push the wall shut behind me and hear the kids go by in the stairwell.

Between the courtyard and me are the kids. I must be there in time or I'll pay a stiff price. But if I venture out I know I will get caught by the kids. I decide to stay put for a bit. Concentrating, I make a small light appear in my hand. I still do not know how I can do this, but I am too afraid to tell anyone. I am ridiculed as it is. I see no reason to give them more reason to be mean. Looking past the walls of my prison, I lean back wondering if it will ever stop.

In the stairway I can hear the pounding of running feet go past down the stairs. Maybe I can make it to the courtyard before they catch me, I hope! Quietly, I move the small part of the wall inwards, poking my head out I look up and down the stairs. I do not see anyone. Slowly, I climb out of my hiding place. Quickly closing the section of wall, I hurry down the stairs and make my way down to the courtyard. Seeing no one in sight, I run as fast as I can to Heastins tower across the courtyard.

Bursting into the room, Heastin looks up from the fire and motions me over to him. Without warning, he hits me in the stomach. "Well boy, you're late. What do you have to say for yourself? I swear by the Weldon council you are helpless".

Lying on the floor, I try to catch my breath. He roughly grabs me and hauls me to my feet. "What have you got to say for yourself Ranwulf? I heard about the fuss you made in class today. You think the others will be hard on you. You will learn what it means to pay for your actions!"

Without fully realizing what is going on, Heastin grabs me by the shirt and drags me outside. In the courtyard all the kids from class are gathered next the well. Heastin drags me in the middle, shoving me to the ground.

"Look, I brought a present for everyone." Looking down at me, Heastin kicks me in the stomach before walking to the edge of the crowd. Through tears, I see everyone gaping at me with glees of pleasure on their faces. Thinking of all the times they have been mean, I resolve I will not let them see me cry or sob. I slowly stand up and look for a way to escape. Seeing none I realize that I have to take what is meted out. Bringing my head up, I turn and look Heastin in the eyes. Heastin looks around motioning to one, he points to me and yells "Well, what are you waiting for Beridon, teach him the first law." Slowly, Beridon moves into the center and approaches me. Holding his hand out in a gesture of peace, he walks towards me. I slowly relax thinking maybe it will not be so bad after all. I watch him move a couple feet away from me without striking me then the next thing I know I am on the ground with a bloody nose, blood flowing down my tunic. Looking up, I see Beridon standing over me. "Come on Ranwulf, get up and at least fight me". Slowly I come to my feet wiping the blood with my sleeve and turn my back on him. "You're not worth it Beridon" I mutter. Heastin calls out to me from the crowd. "What did you say you little outlander" I look up at Heastin with plaintive eyes; in his eyes I see no pity. "Beridon, You are not worth it Beridon, let me walk away and go home" With eyes bulging he stands back from me and looks to Heastin with a question on his lips. "No Beridon, he has not learned yet, finish it." Without warning Beridon knocks me down and starts pummeling me mercilessly. Seeing spots in my vision everything begins to go dark. When I come out of my daze, I see Beridon being held back by the group of kids. Heastin is standing over me, with a scowl on his face.

Everyone backs up a few steps giving me the room to get to my feet. "You did well Ranwulf, not once did you fight back and strike your enemies, maybe you are making progress after all?"

Heastin asks me "What is our first law, Ranwulf?" I look into his eyes and recite the law, "Never strike back at those that strike you." Looking around at the others, he asks them, "Do you think he has learned the second law yet?" All of them look at me and say, "Let him say it Master Heastin!" Looking at me Heastin responds, "Well, you little outlander Ranwulf, What is the second law?" I look straight in front of me and recite the law, "Think of your actions before you act." Pacing around the group Heastin stops and turns toward me, "Does anyone think Ranwulf has been taught a lesson of the second law?" Walking to the front an older boy almost to the age of a hunter speaks up. "Yes, Master Heastin he has been taught a lesson of the second law, I think he will stop before he daydreams in class again, if he does not then we will teach him another lesson!"

The sun is slowly gliding over the tops of the mountains, biting cold winds swirl over the battlements bringing new flurries of snow down on us. Master Heastin dismisses the group of children. Coming up to me, he pushes and shoves me towards the tower he occupies. Swiftly moving in front, I go through the door, I hurriedly take my place next to the fire. Heastin walks into the room and closes the door roughly. "Well, Ranwulf, do you think you are learning our ways at least somewhat?" Staring at the floor not wanting to provoke him more than I have, I answer, "Master, I am learning the ways of our people." Looking at me with those deep silvery eyes Heastin responds, "We will see, you have a lot to learn about us, youngling, our ways are far different from your barbaric origins you were brought up with. I trust in the council's decision, though in my duties to teach you. I swear either you will learn our ways or you will not be alive to learn them."

Heastin walks over the fire and stands next to me, I feel his gaze on me. Slowly, I look up at him and meet his eyes without flinching. "Yes Master?" I ask as I feel dread come upon me. Heastin looks away and responds to my question "Ranwulf, You have been brought to us, but we do not know why. Do you know why we have you living among us; the king says we must teach you our ways. I do not understand why we would teach an outlander our ways, nor do I question the king! Why are you here Ranwulf?" Looking back at the fire, I tell him, "Master Heastin, I do not know, I had hoped over time you would tell me why I am here?" Sitting down in his armchair in front of the fire, Heastin replies, "No, Ranwulf, I don't know, but I will find out, I feel it in my bones that you will lead our people down a dark and dangerous road."

Over the couple of years, life is nothing more than a daily repeat. Every night I go to sleep wishing without hope I knew who I was and why I was brought here. I don't even remember know where I came from or who my family is. The earliest memory I have is waking up years ago in this very bed. I was told by a man in robes that Master Heastin would watch over me and teach me what I needed to know. Since then, every day as been a never ending struggle. All the other kids are told to stay away and not talk to me. I have known for a longtime I am different. One day has I was walking to class I happened to walk by a frozen statue seeing my image reflected back. I look like all the kids except my eyes are brown and not silver, like everyone else. I asked Heastin about it. He just told me to never mind and concentrate on learning. Every night I dream dreams of escaping somewhere.

The only bright spot in my life is making a friend whom I can talk too. One day in class I feel myself falling into one of my spells and I feel a nudge on my shoulder from the boy sitting next to me. I jerk awake and silently thank him for warning me. After the class is out, I feel someone looking at me and see a pretty girl staring at me from across the room before she leaves. I hurry out of the classroom. Looking up and down the hallway, I do not see her and wonder what that meant. I turn around and walk right into her. I stop short and start to apologize, but all I do is stare at the most beautiful image I have seen in my life.

"Well, aren't you going to apologize for stepping on my foot, and if you don't mind," she continues without breathing, "Will you please take your foot off of mine?" I quickly move my foot off hers and stammer an apology, though it comes out like gibberish. "I'm sorry I don't speak your tongue, if that was language?" I cannot stop staring at her and slowly move aside as she moves past me. "By the way my name is Mariale; you should learn to talk before you step on people's feet!"

Not sure exactly what happened I turn away and start walking towards the courtyard as I hear a voice. "Hey, wait up" I turn and see the boy that nudged me in class walking down the corridor. Still a little startled by what happened I stand there and wait for him to catch up. "Friend you looked like you just got slapped by a darsk!" taken back by someone calling me friend I look closer at him. He is a good four inches taller than I am with blond hair and freckles that would put a red head to shame. He is smiling at me with bright silvery eyes, a crooked smile on his face. "Yes, Mariale has had the same effect on me from the first moment I laid eyes on her. Offering his hand, he says, "My name is Balian, What's yours?"

I take his hand shaking it, "My name is Ranwulf, she is beautiful Balian, I could never hope to be with someone like that," stepping back Balian looks me over. "Ranwulf, I know things have not been pleasant for you, but from the sound of your voice, it seems that you have given up." Looking around the corridor looking to make sure no one can hear us. "No, Balian I haven't given up, I just find it easier to go along with others, why?" Balian leans closer saying in a whisper. "If you truly mean that, than meet me at the inner courtyard tonight about two hours after dark." Quickly Balian walks down the corridor and is out of sight before I can say anything.

I hurry to Master Heastins tower and offer myself up to the evening lesson. "No Ranwulf, There will be a lesson later tonight, after I get back. I have a meeting with the council tonight." Swiftly Heastin makes his way out of the door. Looking around the room, I see meat and bread lying on the table. Feeling hungry, I sit down at the table; for once thankfully, I can eat without being taunted. Afterwards, I walk over to the fire and lay down on the hearth. I set there slowly dropping off to sleep. When a log snaps and crackles in the heat, I remember what Balian told me.

I sit up and wonder what time it is, Maybe, I'm not too late to meet Balian in the inner courtyard. I get up and put my wool cloak on heading out the door I make my way along the wall towards the center of the castle. Slowly moving my way into the inner courtyard and see Balian hiding next to a wall in an alcove in the wall, he waves me over. "I thought you would forget about me, come along and you will hear and see things most of us will never witness!" Walking into the castle, we climb the stairs towards my hiding place and as I think we will pass it Balian stops and pushes on the same part of the wall I always do. Looking back he says "Don't look so surprised, Ranwulf, we know of your hiding place, don't worry we won't tell anyone, I see Balian climb into the small space and whisper to him "Balian we both won't fit in there."

Reaching out for my hand Balian pulls me into the wall. Wondering how we could possibly fit into the small space, I climb through the wall. In amazement, I see a passage leading to the right and left. "The hiding place you found is just a small part of the castle. Many passages go from here to different parts of the castle, I will show you them when we have time, but tonight follow me and stay close". It's dark, though I can sense Balians presence in front of me. We seem to be crawling for a while when I feel the passage go downward and in the distance I see a light coming through the wall.

Crawling along the passage I notice it seems to be getting lighter up ahead Balian stops and turning around close to my face he whispers in my ear he says, "No matter what you hear or see do not let our presence be known, do you understand?" Looking at Balian not knowing what to expect I just nod back at him. Slower than before, we creep to the bright spot in the passage. Light is spilling out of a large crack in the rock wall. Balian crawls underneath the opening to the other side and motions me to come forward. Crawling up to the opening in the wall Balian looks through it and motions me to follow his gaze.

Looking through the crack in the wall, far below I see a room with many richly dressed figures. The figures are facing a large jeweled throne sitting on a dais. The back of the throne is high backed with the head of a wolf carved into it. Two magnificently jeweled swords hang below the wolf head, the points meeting just below it. It looks like a thing almost alive. I can almost feel the power of it from this far away. No one is moving or talking in the room, as if they are waiting for a lightning strike right before it happens. A figure stands up in the room. I see Lord Melcore coming forward and raising his hands to the ceiling. I hear his voice like it was from a thousand miles away. "My Lord, We are here at the appointed time, what is your bidding?" Slowly bright white light envelopes the room, being forced to turn away as my eyes water in pain from the brightness, when I can see, once again I look back into the crack to the room and see the most amazing sight I have ever witnessed. On the chair is a man with dark brown hair; with broad shoulders, but what catches my eyes is not the golden and black armor or the jeweled sword, but his face. It is almost as I am looking in a mirror and seeing myself, yet older by years.

With a deep rich voice, the figure on the chair responds to his question. "Yes Heastin, I am here, I have brought you here for a purpose, but first tell me, how does Ranwulf fare?" Looking upon the resplendent figure in gold Heastin kneels before him. "Lord, Ranwulf is difficult at best; we have all but given up on teaching him the ways of our people". Looking out over the figures gathered to hear the words of their leader from ages past, the man in the chair stands up and Ranwulf sees silver sparks shimmering along his armor. His voice booming inside the passage as if thunder has struck all around them, "No, Heastin, How dare you to presume to throw him to the side and move on to another."

Seeming to grow with each word, his wrath becoming more evident with every breath, the kingly figure stands. The power emanating from him knocks all in the chamber to the floor. When it seemed he could not grow any taller he commands them.

"Listen to me well, my people! Teach him the old ways of our people, this must be done. If not you will see your world undone; our people wasting away, slowly crumbling into nothing. Our people will be lost amongst the winds of time if you do not teach him to lead our person, which is his destiny."

Slowly as if the weight of the world was upon his shoulders, Heastin stands up. With his shoulders being weighed down, Heastin looks full into the eyes of the figure standing in front of the throne and says "Lord, you have lead us through peril after peril, but tonight you have shown your weakness. What is the importance of one boy over our people? He is a bane to our people. We will not follow you any longer. The council leads us now. Your time is long past and we will not listen to you again. The council has spoken!" Standing up in the room twelve figures walk to the throne and face their Lord. With hands outstretched, they weave a spell around him and in a few moments breathe the king vanishes from sight. With the passing of their king from sight, they feel a shudder in the walls as the castle shakes. A lone voice issues from everywhere. Bode my word well Melcore. Ranwulf is destined to be High King and nothing you try will stop his destiny from being fulfilled. A great wind fills the throne room as the council cowers on the floor in fear of their lives. Over the walls silvery webs of crackling energy flows.

Ranwulf collapses in the passage, not able to catch his breath. Balian sits there stunned, neither knowing, nor understanding what has happened. The raw power is more than he can take at once. Balian starts moving around first. While Ranwulf sits against the wall trying to make sense of what has happened. Memories flood back from times past, enveloping his mind, seeming to shatter upon him like waves on rocks. He is stunned into unconsciousness. In his mind, he sees great battles fought, armies clashing together. The screams of the dying reverberate across the times. For ages, the battles continue, and then he is floating above an empty field. After a time, two peoples meet in the center of the field. One he sees is the Weldons. They are a fair race; most have light skin and dark hair. They dress in light armor, wearing swords and wielding bows of wood. On the other side of the field are the Melcaren people. They are a darker skin people, wearing furs and wielding sharp, battle-axes, with wicked curved swords hanging from their backs. With a glint in their eyes, they come to the treatise table wearing their weapons.

The Weldons are forced off their lands and flee north over the mountains into the cold, harsh lands. As they flee north, they encounter the Turiec people, a hard and bitter race living in the northern mountains. Caught between enemies, they fight for their lives. The leader of the turiec fights a bitter war, slowly giving up land a foot at a time. But, slowly, the Weldons prevail against them. In a final battle, Meroth is thrown down by King Roanoled. The King banishes the Turiec people to the far bitter northern wastelands. With his last stand against the Weldon King Meroth swears an oath that he and his people will not rest until the Weldons are destroyed.

Many of the Weldons die the first winter, before they can build houses and fight off the new enemies. Monsters from stories and legends are among them. The cold and the hunger meet them at every step. The Weldons that survive through the first winter learn to live in the bitter waste, but over time, Ranwulf sees his people growing less and less. Fewer of his people are born, they do not continue their culture as in times past, and it is just a fight to survive. Amongst the people, the great council comes into being. At first, the council was a force for the people.

Nevertheless, over time they grow away from the old ways and teach the new Weldons the promise of peace and flight, no longer will others kill their people. They will live here in the cold waste and survive. For if they keep the great mountains between them and the other races, no more will die a violent death.

Ranwulf sees his people slowly dying; now understanding why he is here. In the distant recesses of his mind, he hears a voice calling his name, again with more force he hears this voice and goes towards it. He feels someone shaking him. He wakes up abruptly seeing Balian in the dark leaning over him. "Ranwulf, are you Alright?"

Looking around to see where he is Ranwulf sits up, and in the palm of his hand a light glows brightly. Seeing the fright in Balians eyes, Ranwulf sends out to his mind a calming thought. "Yes, Balian, I now understand what must be done and thank you for bringing me here tonight". Hearing a movement back in the tunnel Ranwulf, puts the light out and holds onto Balians shoulder keeping him still. Every now and again, they can hear a scuffle and a movement coming towards them.

When it seems the noise is almost on top of them, Ranwulf causes the light to blaze in his hand. In the bright light, the two see Mariale holding her arm across her eyes. Quickly Ranwulf dims the light and says to Mariale, "what are you doing, why are you here?' Looking behind me, she looks toward Balian. "Good Balian you're here too, Ranwulf you must flee quickly, the council has called for your arrest, the guards are searching everywhere for you".

In desperation she grabs his shoulders, shaking them "Ranwulf are you listening, we must flee, the council has called for you to be brought to them!"

"Mariale, how can we flee, we have nowhere to go?" Looking at me impatiently, Mariale says, "We don't have time to talk, Balian where does this tunnel lead to?" Moving closer to talk in a whisper Balian motions the way they were going "As far as I have been down the tunnel, I think it goes below the castle, I went as far as some caverns, but stopped and came back before exploring much of them; I can show us the way there". Putting her hand on Ranwulf knee Mariale pleads, "Ran, we must go and flee as quickly as we can before they discover which way we went!" Taking her hand Ranwulf says, "I don't know what's going on, but I don't want to go back to the castle ever, all I want to do is get out of here".

With Balian taking the lead, they slowly wind their way through the narrow tunnel. After what seemed like hours, the tunnel opened up to a height, which made walking easier. Keeping the light dim they moved slowly through the tunnel, but every so often they could hear voices on the other side of the wall, Ran was worried about too much light, fretting someone could see it. The tunnel kept going down and winding along at what seemed a Random direction. After a couple hours of walking, they reached an open area in the tunnel that proved to be a large room with a door in the middle of each wall.

Letting the light flare a little brighter Ran looked at each door. "Balian which way do we go?" when neither Mariale nor Balian answers him, he looks at them, "Alright what is going on here," Ran demands at his whits end. Balian looks to Mariale, "Mariale it is time to tell him."

Mariale faces Ranwulf, "Ran, We have been watching you for a long time now, wondering when the council would move against you." Joining in Balian says, "Yes Ran we know the council fears you and thinks you will be the destruction of our people, we don't think so."

Staring back and forth between them, "I don't understand what everyone is talking about, all I know is I was brought here and have been just trying to survive."

Sitting against the wall Ranwulf says, "Why would either of you want to go anywhere with me?" Putting his hands on his lap, Ranwulf looks up at Mariale. "All I have done the last year is get in trouble and make everyone around me miserable."

"Ran, I don't know exactly where we will be led by you but, I see hope for our people in you," Mariale says as she kneels next to him. Balian comes to stand in front of them. "Ranwulf, I would not run from my home and take a chance of bringing the councils fury upon me if I didn't see hope for us in you!" Mariale grabs hold of Ranwulfs hand "Ran, we must go, but it is up to you which way we go."

Looking at them both Ranwulf, stands up feeling new resolve flow into him. Walking across the room Ranwulf looks back and motions toward the door straight ahead. "Let us go, we need to get away before someone finds us, Balian, where does this door lead too?" Looking at Ranwulf, Balian responds. "I don't know Ranwulf I have only been this far." Looking at his friends Ranwulf tells them, "There is only one way to find out." Turning around Ranwulf leads his friends down the door and into a new future.

Chapter Two
Heritage Revealed

The friends walk down the winding tunnel going deeper into the earth. The walls seem to hold its own warmth. Walking for what seemed like hours, they come into a large cavern. The three abruptly stop at the entrance looking on into the cavern. Carvings from ages past cover the walls. The floor is smoothly paved with great flagstones colored in grey. Ranwulf looks into the room, amazed by the carvings that blend in to the ceiling, for the ceiling seems to open up into a star-studded sky. Though dim, the light is bright after walking through the tunnels with only a small light to lead them. In the center of the room is a fountain carved into the form of six wolves facing each other with the statue of a man in the center wearing armor, raising a sword to the sky, water is flowing from the wolves' mouths filling the basin.

With a barely audible whisper, Ranwulf stammers, "What is this place?" Looking around Mariale responds, "I learned when I was younger that below the castle are the old ruins from ages past, we must have found them!" Ranwulf starts walking into the room looking at everything, "Come on, let's look around and see what's down here." The other two walk into the room staying close to each other.

"I am thirsty," Balian says. He walks over to the fountain and slowly dips his hand in drinking the cold clear water. The other two take suit and slack their thirst. Looking around Balian says "If this is the old ruins no one has been here in thousands of years, I can't believe this has lasted that long!" Walking around and looking at the carvings Balian points to one and exclaims "Look, this is a picture of our people fighting a battle." Coming up to him Ranwulf looks over the carving and see's two peoples facing each other across a plain. They are armored and rushing on horseback to meet each other, weapons drawn. He can almost hear the battle cries from long ago.

Turning around Ranwulf sees Mariale standing in front of the statue in the center of the fountain. "Who do you two think this is?" coming up to her, they look at the figure Ranwulf replies, "I don't know Mariale, but I feel I should know him. I don't understand why."

Giving the room one last glimpse they walk towards the hallway at the far side of the cavern. Walking along the hallway the same starry night follows the ceiling wherever they go. "Which way should we go?" Balian asks. They can see many doorways along the hallway. "I don't know Balian, let's pick one and see where it takes us," Ranwulf responds.

Taking a doorway that leads down a stairway, they make their way deeper into the ruins. Carvings are everywhere along the walls. Images of feasting and gatherings, Pictures of long forgotten battles dot the walls. Even lone figures dressed in battle armor or plain clothes. Coming to the end of the staircase the three friends find themselves in a winding corridor leading to a small hall. The corridor dead end going either right or left are the only choices.

"Well, I guess it doesn't matter which way we go, but I think I want to go left from here," Ranwulf says. "Ok, we'll follow you Ran," Mariale responds. Walking along the corridor they see at the end is a large open chamber. Walking up to the doorway, they pause on the threshold and stop looking in amazement at the sight. At the far end of the massive room is a throne set upon a dais raised above the room. The night sky lights the room with stars blazing away in the heavens.

More colors reflect off the high-backed throne than the three have seen in their entire lives. On either side of the throne are two smaller thrones, though not as impressive as the middle one. Looking around the room Ranwulf looks along the walls, suits of armor line the walls. A massive long table is in the center of the room. Walking slowly into the room, he comes up to the table seeing it is a deep rich dark room gilded in gold along the sides.

Turning back to his friends, he motions for his friends to come forward. Looking down at the table he points to golden letters painted into the wood every few feet. Each place has a name on it they have never heard before. One says Turef, then the next Mectuil, on and on down the table.

"Who do you think they are?" asks Ranwulf. "I don't know, I have never heard those names before, have you Balian." Looking around when Balian does not respond they see him at the bottom of the steps looking at the thrones.

Hurrying towards him Ranwulf says, "What do you think of this place, friend?" Turning around with a light in his eyes, Balian points to the throne "Ranwulf, look at the high throne, tell me what you see?" feeling Mariale at his side Mariale exclaims, "Ran look at the throne!" Looking up Ranwulf starts walking up the dais and cannot believe his eyes. Slowly reverently walking up to the throne he kneels down in front of it, looking at the top of the back of the chair. What he sees leaves him breathless. For, in golden letters written for everyone to see is his name. High King Ranwulf! Looking back at his friends "What is this? Why is my name written on there?" Slowly Balian and Mariale walk up to the throne and kneels down behind Ranwulf laying her hand on his shoulder. "Ranwulf, I don't know what this means. Balian, do you?"

Balian responds, "No, I don't know what it means but I think it is a sign Ranwulf, what is that?" looking on the side of the throne Ranwulf spots a horn hung off the armrest. Taking the horn in his hand, he looks at it closely. Upon the sides of the horn are runes and carvings in shapes he does not understand. "What are these, do you think?' he says. Looking closer at the horn Baliansays, "I don't know, but I feel it was meant for you."

Standing up Ranwulf takes the horn and looks back down towards the doorway across the room. Without knowing why, he brings the horn to his lips and sounds it. Balian and Mariale come to their feet in an instant alarmed at the thunderous noise. "Ranwulf, why…" Balian starts to ask then stops as the three friends see a light approaching from the hallway.

With nowhere to go, they simply stand there waiting for the light to approach. In the distance they see a group of figures approaching across the room, they are richly dressed. In the front is a splendid figure fully armored, a jeweled long sword at his waist. Waiting for the figures to approach, they see them stop at the bottom of the stairs. The only one that continues towards them is the leader.

Slowly, he climbs the stairs to the throne and stops a few feet away looking at Ranwulf.

"Ranwulf, you have called upon the horn of gathering. We have been waiting for you for ages." Not knowing what to say Ranwulf looks at the man asking, "Who are you and why have you been waiting for me?"

"Do you not already know in your heart whom I am Son?" feeling as if he has been struck by lightning, Ranwulf steps back and looks at the man "Father?" He stammers. "Yes, my son we have waited for the time to approach, have your dreams not spoken to you," the figure says. Responding to him, Ranwulf stammers "Yes, my dreams have been strange of late; though I thought what I saw was nothing more than a dream."

"No, Ranwulf we have met before though you may not remember for some time to come. In time you will remember."

Looking at his father Ranwulf asks "Father, why have you brought me here?" Ranwulf asks. Looking somberly at me he answers, "No, you must find your own way. For now, you must flee from our people and grow into the man you are to become. You have a strong deep heritage in you. You must go out among the people of the world and learn. When the appointed time is near we will meet again and you will take your place. Look towards the isle across the sea, you will find yourself and your birthright there."

With a sad slow smile, the figures in the room disappear like wisps of smoke upon the wind, in a matter of moments only the three friends are standing in the great room. Sitting heavily down on the throne Ranwulf stares across the room wishing he did not feel so alone.

Sitting down at the top of the stairs, they look around the room. "Well, what do we do know? I haven't got the foggiest idea where to go or in the least how to get out of here?" Ran asks Mariale.

Mariales responds, "Ok, first we need to get out of here and head to somewhere that we can find answers." Balian looks up at the sky overhead and stands up, "I for one would like to feel the sun on my back without wearing layers of clothes just to keep warm." Walking down the stairs, he looks back, "Are you two just going to sit around and turn into statues?"

"No, Balian, but answer me a question, why are you doing this?" looking at them both Ran wonders at his new friends. "Why are you both doing this, you are leaving everything you know." Mariale looks into Ranwulfs eyes, "Ran, I felt from the moment I saw you that our futures were intertwired, when I see you I see the heart of our people. I can't explain it any better than that."

Balian looks again at the ceiling, "Ranwulf have you ever looked up at the sky and wondered if there was a better life out there, I mean somewhere else? Well, I have and I see our people are wondering the same thing. In time they will need a leader and in you I see that leader."

"Alright, then if I'm not in a dreaming all this, then let's find our way out of here and go south. I have never been there, but I know I need to look for the isle across the great sea. Until then I think we should explore the lands and learn what we can."

Walking down the stairs the three friends make their way out of the room, heading back up the hallways towards the nearest corridor. Coming upon the hallway that brought them down here, they go straight. Walking along the corridor, they see a light ahead, a bright light that is a color that none of them have ever seen before. A cold wind is blowing towards them. Turning a corner of the hall, they have to shield their eyes from the bright sunlight coming from an open window. Ranwulf walks to the window and looks out, standing there he is amazed at the scene below him.

It feels almost as if they are flying as they stand there overlooking great mountains below. Snow covers them almost down to the roots. In the distance, looking down they can see great rivers flowing out of the hills far below. At his shoulder, Mariale points far out in the distance. "What is that, Ran?" Looking to where she points, they see great expanses of green to the south, then heading east huge areas of lighter green flatlands. "That I think is the lands of the peoples of the south, I had no idea!" Balian looks over the ledge of the window "So how do we get from here to there, you two, I certainly can't fly?"

"What do you think Ran, Where do we go from here, now that we have seen which way we want to go?" With a last look through the window, Ranwulf turns away and looks down the corridor, "I assume we should find out where this goes and start moving down at all possible turns."

I do not see any other alternatives. We need to get out of here soon; we need food and water," Balian says. Ran, takes the prompt moves down the hall looking for stairs or corridors. After walking for some time they find a circular stairway, a light flows out from Ranwulfs hand as he peers down the stairs. "Sometime Ran you will have to explain how you do that," Mariale says. Without responding Ranwulf leads the way down. For what seems like ages, the friends make their way down the stairs. "It feels warmer you two," Balians says.

"It's been getting warmer; I've been sweating for a while," Mariale responds. "Ok, let's just find a way out of here," Ranwulf admonishes them. "Balian is just getting tired and cranking Ran." Mariale teases Balian. Coming to the bottom of the stairs, they see a corridor leading away to the right into the distance. "We need to stop some place here for a while and get some rest. I don't think we will make it down in one try." Ran says. "I think it will take some time to get down there. We need to figure out the quickest way out of here, we'll be needing food and warmth soon," Balian replies. "How are we going to get food you two? We did not bring any weapons or hunting tools. I have a knife on me but that won't do much good," Mariale asks them. "Let's just get out of here and then we can worry about stuff later, I for one am not going back for mine," Ran says as he heads down the hall.

Walking down the hall Balian and Mariale catches up with Ranwulf as he comes to an open doorway. Looking through they see another staircase heading down and to the right. Looking back at them Ran heads down the staircase. "Let's try to get lower and see if it is warmer before we stop for a rest."

They trod down the stairs for the next couple of hours in silence. Coming to a lower hallway, they sit on the bottom step, rubbing stiff and sore muscles. "It is getting warmer," Balian says while he takes off his outer cloak. Ranwulf lowers his hood and feeling the warmer air he stands up with a groan of protesting muscles. "I am sore now, I feel as if we've walked forever! Let us rest here for a while and see what the morning brings, if morning it is?'

"I for one can't walk another step!" Mariale groans. Laying down on the bottom step, she is asleep before the other two can blink. "Balian, get some rest. When I can't stay awake I'll wake you up," Ran says as he stands up and slowly walks around. "Make sure you do Ran, we have no idea what's down here."

After a few minutes, Ranwulf ventures a little way down the hall, seeing nothing he goes back to his friends and sits down. For a few hours, Ranwulf sits and thinks of the last couple of days. His life has changed drastically the last few years. Resolving to make the best of it, he stands back up and nudges the others awake. "Come on, let's make a run for it and get out of here." Bleary eyed they sit up. Almost immediately, Mariale's muscles are cramped and unforgiving. "I feel like I've been beaten half to death!" she complains.

"The sooner you get moving Mariale the quicker your muscles will straighten out." Balian mutters through his own pain. With grumbling stomachs and stiff legs, they make their way down the hallway towards room at the end. Walking through the opening of the room, they look around and see a couple long tables arranged down the walls next to a set of windows looking out into the dark sky. The friends walk over to the windows wanting to see the land below. "In the dark I can't see much except we have come down a lot with the stairs help," Ranwulf observes. "I can't see anything except a lot of stars; I do feel a warm breeze though," Mariale says. Walking away from the windows, Balian looks back, "We aren't down yet, and we have some distance to go before we get to the plains below."

"Let's follow one of these doors and see where it goes," Suggests Ranwulf. Walking across the room, they pick the opening closest to them and start the last trek to the lands below. After a few hours of walking down stairs and through a maze of rooms and interconnecting corridors, the three friends come upon two heavily barred doors. They are easily each ten feet wide, and twenty feet tall enough for five men to walk abreast of each other. Looking at the massive bar holding them shut, Ranwulf and Balian look for a way to move it. "It is too heavy for us to lift, how do we get it out of the way?" Balian mutters. Looking around the room Ranwulf sees a chain coming down from the ceiling from the darkness. "Balian, help me with this." Reaching up the two grab the chain and slowly pull down.

With the creaking of long unused metal, the bar slowly moves. In a few pulls of the chain, they hear a loud click and the bar stays in place. Almost upon their own, the two doors silently swing open, letting the bright daylight inside.

Shying away from the opening, creeping to the side they look out the entrance. No more than ten feet ahead is a tall stonewall. Looking up they can see the sun far above, in a clear light blue sky. "Hey Look the clouds are gone!' Mariale exclaims. Together the three go through the entrance and start looking at the walls, trying to see a way to go from there. Suddenly with a clash the great doors slam shut. Jumping back towards them they hear the bar slam down and feel the door vibrate with the violence of it. "Well, we can't turn back now" Balian notices bluntly. With an exasperated look, Mariale rolls her eyes towards the sky. "Really, you don't say Balian." She turns around and notices a path leading to the right of the wall. "Why didn't we see that before?" she wonders aloud.

"I don't know Mariale, but if it's a way out, I plan on taking it," they hear Ranwulf say as he walks away.

Chapter Three
The Search Begins

"What are you talking about?" Melcore demands of Heastin, biting off each word with a snap of his mouth. Melcore raises his fist at Heastin, "He got away! The boy got away he says! Why of all the dumb, stupid, darsk things I have ever heard in my life! I can plainly see that he got away!"

"My Lord, we tried to intercept him after the council, I went to get the others and when…" sharply cutting him off Melcore slaps Heastin in the mouth, "I don't want to hear your excuses Heastin. If we do not find that little blubbering fool, we will all pay for it. Do you hear me? I have to go now, meet me up in the north tower later tonight. At least find out which way he got out of here." Muttering under his breath, he storms off.

Standing up from the floor, Heastin wipes the blood from his lip. Walking quickly out of the room and down the hall Heastin stops the first servant he sees. "You, go find Derhuick, tell him to meet me in my tower." Almost running Heastin starts thinking of the ways out of the castle, quickly thinking of the short time past, since they lost him Heastin starts narrowing down which way he could have gone. Opening the door to the lower chamber Heastin is surprised when he sees Derhuick sitting by the fire. "What, How did you get here so quick? Never mind, have you found any trail?"

"No Heastin, I haven't it's like he just disappeared in a puff of smoke." Huddling closer to the fire Derhuick shivers. "This cold here is horrible, how could you live here all the time?" Heastin says. "Be quiet before someone hears you, you have been gone from here for too long." Walking to the fire Heastin sits on the hearth. Heastin looks at Derhuick "Well, have you found anything?"

"No, not a trace, Are you sure he's gone? Maybe he is hiding somewhere in the castle. Derhuick responds. "How could a foolish dolt like Ranwulf get away so quickly?" Heastin mutters to himself. "Heastin I've looked everywhere he could possible hide. Somehow, he got out. Everyone is watching for him, all that can be done, is being done, until this storm breaks. My scouts cannot go out in this blinding storm until it slacks off abit. If he's out there he is will be frozen solid by morning."

The door abruptly opens interrupting any further conversation. Melcore screams from the doorway "What in the councils name are you doing here sitting by the fire, while the plague of our people is making his escape?" shocked Heastin jumps up "We're getting ready to make another search through the castle Lord."

"Heastin, I'm sending you and a few scouts north through the pass to try to find him. The council hasn't been able to locate him." Coming over to the fire Melcore looks at Derhuick closely. "Heastin, go meet the scouts by the north gate the sooner we start looking outside the castle the quicker we can find him. Now Go!" Heastin quickly grabs his heaviest furs and light weapons heading out the door. "Derhuick, come sit down for a minute, we need to speak." Looking around the room at the odds and ends thrown about Melcore looks closer at Derhuick. "How much time have you spent in the southern lands?" Looking into the fire Derhuick responds. "Lord, for the last few years, I've hardly been back here. I would still be there if not for your summons."

"Well then, what would you say if you could live there for the rest of your life, without being summoned back here? Looking at MelcoreDerhuick wonders at the thought "Lord, how could that be?"

"If you find the boy and bring him back to us, the council has declared you free and may return unhindered to the south. You have had success in the past finding others who escaped there. I don't understand your motives for wanting to live among the Melcaren people, but if you do this you will save your people from utter destruction." Standing up Derhuick says, "Lord, Even if you haven't offered me this choice I would still bring this boy back. Our people are too weak to fight the southern nation. None better than I know the threat the southerns are."

"Gather together thirty of your scouts and be ready to leave at first light. I want you to be the one to bring him back. Therefore, you fully know the councils intentions in this. Alive or dead, I want him brought back. Just stop him and the road he goes down!" Kneeling before Melcore, Derhuick pledges to him "In this I will not fail my lord, either way he will be brought back for judgment!"

Standing over Derhuick, Melcore scowls down at him "Do not fail me in this Derhuick or you will wish I had killed you here and now." Swiftly, Melcore leaves. Sitting back in the chair Derhuick thinks of the southern lands far below and the sun shining on his back again. "Yes, it will be good to get back down south and away from the cold." If one boy thinks he will stop him from claiming his prize, this Ranwulf will be surprised.

Heastin quickly walks to the northern gate. Coming around the upper courtyard he sees twenty-five of his scouts gathered. Melcore is standing to the side quietly talking to the guards. Seeing Heastin arrive, Melcore abruptly cuts off his conversation and walks to the front of the gathered scouts. Heastin quickly approaches Melcore coming to stand at his side. "Master, as you commanded twenty of my handpicked scouts have been assembled. We await your orders." Looking around at the men Melcore scowls back at Heastin; walking closer to

MICHAEL RANDOLPH

the men Melcore addresses them. "Men, we have had a boy escape from the castle this night. I chose you for your loyalty and hardiness. You must track him down and bring him back to us. This boy you pursue is not like any others in the past." Walking back to Heastin he turns around facing the squad of scouts. "His only route of escape from us is to the Findeild fence across the northern waste. Search our northern lands and find him! The council commands that he is to be brought back for questioning or his body is to be brought back."

Looking straight into Heastins eyes, Melcore gives his last command, "Do not fail in this search; do not come back until you have him in your possession!"

Looking around at the majestic walls of the castle, Heastin draws his shoulders back, holding his head high he turns away from Melcore. Immediately the scouts come alert. Without another word, the scouts follow Heastin out of the massive gates. Heastin breaks into a slow dogged run. He feels eyes upon him as they crest the top of the first hill leading away from the great castle. Knowing that Melcore is standing upon the parapet looking down he travels onward until the squad is out of view of the castle. Turning up a hill and following the ravine down a few yards, he stops, motioning for his men to come closer.

Heastin motions for Hurest and Nuirc to follow him a few feet away. "Listen you two, we have a long trek ahead of us and need to catch this boy as quick as we can. We need to find a place to shelter for the cold bitter night coming on first and then a few of us can go out and locate his trail."

"I know a good place to stop for a bit," Hurest says. "Show us Hurest" Heastin responds. The men walk down the road a few hundred feet turning off it at an ice tree. Coming around the backside of the massive ice tree, they see an opening in the back with a slope leading down into it. Following Hurest the

38

squad moves down the slope into the tree. After a few feet, they turn a corner and walk into a room lined with benches along the wall, plenty of room for the men to sleep.

"Hurest, Nuirc come here." Heastin beckons to the center of the room. It will most likely take a day or two to find his trail in the snowstorm, let us send out a couple scouts with each of us and start looking. Hurest picks out two men and swiftly leaves the tree, heading back into the ice and snow.

Nuirc motions two of his scout to the exit and quickly heads out. Heastin motions for one of the men to come over "Feruch, I will meet you outside in a moment, we have a long night ahead of us." Feruch quickly walks back up the sloped entrance disappearing into the driving snow. "Men, set up camp, but be ready to leave in a moments time if need be." Heastin says as he walks into the gathering night. Coming up the slope Heastin can barely see Feruch in the driving snow and ice. Heastin motions for him to follow as he walks around the tree.

Loping down the road a small distance, they stop by the side of an ice field. Not being able to see anything for more than ten feet, Heastin motions for Feruch to stay on the other side of the road as they start scanning for any sign. Almost crab like, the two men are bent double from walking in the driving ice and blowing wind. Coming around a corner in the road, by wind and ice assaulted them. Heastin crawls over to Feruch handing him the end of a rope, he motions for him to tie it around his waist.

After tying the other end to his waist, they head into the storm intent on finding their prey.

Melcore strides back to the northern tower. He is fuming, furious about losing Ranwulf. Thinking of any possible places for the boy to be hiding or which way he could have gotten away. Scrying for him has come to no avail; it would be easier to find where melted snow had gone.

Melcore approaches his massive tower, looking up he sees the carven sculptures in the walls. The Weldons rebuilt this castle after they came to this barren land. Over the ages, the sculptures have been entombed in layers of ice. Carven into the rock are lions, hippogriffs' with long hooked claws, wyverns flying over armored men on horseback. Battles are being played out behind the ice, Golden armored warriors in pitched battle on fields of valor in places long forgotten. The tops of the towers and battlements had long become disused as ice incased them, growing steadily upwards until the whole castle looked as if it was a mighty bastion of trees made out of ice entrapping a race of people.

His people had try to keep their heritage alive, but over the ages, just like the ice his culture had slowly grown away from any thought except the battle to survive. The prophecies said this boy was destined to bring them back into the world. They would not survive an onslaught from the southern kingdoms, as had happened when they were exiled to this land. He would hunt down this boy before he would witness his people destroyed.

Entering the north tower Melcore quickly climbed the stairs. He hears voices at the top go silent as the council sees Melcore enter the chamber. "The scouts are on the hunt." He tells the council. "We have attempted to locate the boy, but he is hidden from us." Feal says. "He is being protected it seems." Melcore replies, "We will have to attempt other ways to find him, the scouts are on the way north and south tonight. He could not have traveled far in a couple hours." From the stairs, the sound of running feet can be heard. Through the door a disheveled woman appears, followed by a guard. "Lord, she would not be gainsaid, as soon as I opened the door she flew past me," the guard stutters.

Running up to Melcore the woman drops to the ground, breathing heavily from the climb. "Lord...My Mariale...She's gone....we can't ...find her anywhere." Bending down and helping the woman to her feet, Melcore leads her over to a chair by the fire. Lwuilerest quickly gets up from the chair taking the woman's' other hand helping her to sit. Kneeling down in front of her, Melcore pats her hand lightly. Clearing his mind, he lets peaceful thoughts flow to her from his mind. Soon the woman breathes easier and her mind clears. "Now, young woman, tell me what has happened tonight to your daughter," Melcore tells her.

Looking at Melcore she slowly tells him of her fright. "Earlier tonight I went into our family quarter's looking for Mariale after she didn't return home after school; her friends told me she had been gone all day. I Ran back to our rooms and saw she had not been back. I noticed a letter on her bed telling me not to worry and she would be fine. She had to go somewhere, not being able to say where or when she would be back. It said they had to help Ranwulf. What does this mean Lord? What does my little girl have to do with Ranwulf; I have heard the council is looking for him."

Looking to Feal he nods and Feal leaves the room hurriedly. Turning his attention back to the woman, he admonishes her "Now, we just want to talk to Ranwulf, nothing more." Continuing on he says. "We don't know what your precious girl has to do with Ranwulf, but we will find her and bring her home to you." Melcore helps the woman stand to her feet. His arm around her shoulders he guides her to the doorway. "Now, young lady, I suggest you go back to your rooms and help your family to get through this trying time. As soon as we have news of her, we will let you know." Before letting her go with the guard, he turns her around, looking into her eyes Melcore says, "If you hear anything from her or Ranwulf, please let us know as quickly as you can. It is vitally important we talk to Ranwulf. Do you understand dear?"

Looking relieved at the councils concern, she smiles and responds. "I will my lord, I promise if I hear from Mariale I will come straight away to you, thank you Lord Melcore!" Motioning to the guard the woman is led back down the stairs.

"Well, He did have help after all, I knew he couldn't have gotten away so swiftly by himself." Melcore exclaims. Feal comes back into the room and nods to Melcore. "We have found a trace of the girl, though it is faint as if it was from years ago."

"Her being close to the boy must be obscuring your vision Feal," Melcore observes. "Where did you feel the strongest trace at?"

"Near the eastern wall, by the school, though it is strange, I felt her presence moving back and forth under the ground." Feal says. Looking around at the council Melcore responds to her, "They must have found the passages under the castle. I thought I was the only one that knew of them."

Coming to stand in front of MelcoreFeal demands "What passages are those Melcore, why have you hidden their presence from us!" Melcore looks down at her. "Feal, I will not be berated by you; if I chose to keep that knowledge to myself, it is not of your concern. They lead to the old ruins below the castle grounds. It is better that our people do not know of them."

"Yes I agree with you on that account, but we need to know about such things. Take us to the tunnels so we may ferret out these children before they get away," Feal demands. "That is not a good idea Feal, only I may travel the passages, then only at great risk." Melcore walks over to the fire. "The passages are from our distant past, they have gone wild over the ages. You might walk down a corridor and never find your way back. I explored them once and barely came back out alive." Sitting down in his chair, he looks at the councils members.

"I need to think on what to do about this turn of events. Let us meet again in the morning," Melcore says. The council slowly moves out of the room one by one. "Please stay Feal, we need to speak," Melcore says. She comes over to Melcore looking down at him in the chair. "Melcore, hiding knowledge from the council may have cost us dearly. If he has gone down into these ruins as you say, we still need to know which way he has gone in order to bring him back. The council will not rest easy until they have been captured and subdued." Snow falls from the grey foreboding clouds as Melcore looks out his window from the north tower. The night is growing old. Though dawn never comes to this cold barren wasteland, he knows morning is not far off. The need to act rails upon him, making his muscles tense, He feels like a caged animal screaming to be let loose. Turning his attention back to the Feal, he continues the discussion. "Feal, Derhuick is leading his scouts south this morning. You shall accompany them."

Turning away from the fire, coldly staring at MelcoreFeal responds, "Why, would I go with the scouts on a mission to the southern lands, Melcore?"

"Because Feal, it is your duty to see that this boy is captured and brought back to us. Derhuick has been to the southern lands many times, he is the most able among us to travel the lands." Melcore responds. Sitting down at the table, he unrolls a map, waving Feal over to look at it. "This is an old map of the ruins below. It will help guide you. Take it with you, but do not carry it once you find your way through to the lands below, Feal." Melcore instructs her.

"Very well Melcore, I will go with Derhuick to find this boy. Once we have subdued him, I think there will be changes in the council. You have made a mess of this and have shown far less wisdom in these matters than befits the leader of our people." Bristling at the comment Melcore responds, "Feal, fulfill your duty to our people first, once this threat is extinguished then we can discuss the future!" Coming into the room, Derhuick bows to the council. "My scouts are ready for the journey south my lords and lady." Standing up and walking over to DerhuickMelcore instructs the leader of the scouts. "Derhuick, Gather your men down by the eastern wall. From there I will open the gate and put your feet upon the path to the south."

"Yes my Lord." Derhuick quickly retreats down the stairs to gather his men. "Feal, Come with me." Melcore says as he hurries from the chamber. Following the streets across the ancient castle Melcore and Feal cross, the castle coming to a blank ice covered wall on the eastern castle wall. "Do you plan on having us jump over the wall Melcore?" Feal says looking around.

"Just wait and watch Feal, maybe this journey will teach you some wisdom you lack." Melcore stands looking at the ice encrusted wall seeming to lose him-self in thought. Derhuick quietly waits behind the council members. Soon Melcore walks up to the wall speaking in a strange language he traces on an unseen symbol onto the wall of ice. The cracking and splintering of ice can be heard above the blowing wind. Snow slackens its' pace while the cracking of ice gets louder. Standing in amazement, they are amazed as a section of ice splinters away from the wall. "Clear the area of ice," Melcore instructs the scouts.

Quickly moving forward the men move the great slabs of ice, a tunnel through the ice is shown to lead to a small ornately carved image of a door in the wall. "Melcore, what is this?" Feal asks. "This is your way to the ruins below," says Melcore moving forward into the short tunnel. Intoning a word, the outlines of the door flare in bright light. Slowly, the door moves outwards, showing a corridor leading away into the mountainside.

"Feal, stay to the course of the map. Do not stray from it. If you do you, you will never come out of the ruins below." Melcore instructs her. Turning around to Derhuick and his men Melcore looks them over. "Derhuick, I lay upon you the charge to find this boy and return him to the council. Do not fail me in this. Nothing is more important than stopping him!"

"I will not fail you, my lord!" Derhuick motions to his men to begin the journey through the ruins. Melcore stands alone in front of the door as he sees the last of the company disappear through the entrance.

Waving his hands in an intricate pattern the door to the ruins begins to close. Just before the door completely shuts a great, thunderous noise comes bellowing out of the depths of ruins below. Melcore is stunned, his hands freezing as dread is visited upon him hearing the horn of the gathering being winded.

Above him, the call of the horn echoes through the castle bouncing off every wall. With a great splintering and cracking, the eastern wall starts moving and heaving. As Melcore turns to flee, the ice wall buckles, sending great slabs cascading from the heights above. He sees from the corner of his eye the door buckle from the weight of the ice and the wall collapse into the tunnel. Fleeing the flow of ice from above, the last thing Melcore feels before darkness takes him is amazement of the gathering horn being winded.

Chapter Four
The Southern Forest

Looking down the hills from above, the three friends quietly talk amongst themselves. Searching the horizon Ranwulf sees the path going down to the edge of a great forest covered in a thick mist. "How far away do you think the forest is Balian?" Ran asks.

"I'm not sure, but it will take a day or two to reach it at least." Balian looks out over the hills, trying to find the best way down. "If we stay in the ravines, we could make it without being seen, I think." He offers. Mariale is less than happy with more walking before finding food. "It won't matter after a little more time; we need to find food before much longer you two. I'm starving!" Earlier they saw a patrol of soldiers moving along the hills heading west into the morning sun. Having traveled down from the mountains during the night, they had skirted a walled fortress without knowing it. Now the way was blocked to the north and they were hiding and scampering through the hills trying to escape this new threat.

"We can't let them find us. We need to keep moving, maybe if we reach the forest we can find a way through." Ran starts over the rise and drops to the ravine below. Mariale and Balian follow suite in a crablike run down the wash. Throughout the morning they skitter from one ravine to another, resting when they could, while keeping a close eye out for patrols going past. At one point, they hid just under a small overhang while a small patrol passed within feet of them. They could hear the patrol move past almost on top of them. One soldier had said to another, "How long are we going to be out here looking for ghosts?" The leader of the patrol had responded shortly to him. "As long as the reports come in that new activity has been sighted up north. One of the patrols saw three people coming down from the hills last night, but lost them in the dark, now keep a close eye out."

They had been more careful after that, making sure no one was in sight while moving through the low hills and ravines of the mountains. It had become clear that they were considered the enemy and had to get south as quick as they could. The morning had waned into early afternoon when Balian spotted a small trickle of water coming out of the ground as they were passing through a ravine farther down the foothills. Sitting down, the three were filling up on water thinking of their next move.

"We should wait here till nightfall Ran; it will be easier to make our way down as long as the moon is up like last night." Balian says. Looking around closely Ran responds to Balian. "We need a little rest before we move much more anyway. "That's the best idea I've heard today." Mariale says. Mariale moves under a small cliff laying sitting down with her back against the wall. "It's hot here, the sun is blinding me. I will be glad to get into the forest. I feel like the whole world can see us."

Balian walks over to Mariale. "Get some rest you two, I'll wake you up if I hear or see anything." Walking up to the top of the ravine Balian takes a perch by a boulder keeping an eye out for patrols.

With the moonlight shining in his face Ran is startled awake as Balian moves back down the ravine. A shower of loose rocks precedes him. "Alright, its' time to go, a patrol just pasted north of us." He calls softly. Slowly getting to their feet, the three stumble down the ravine into the foothills of the mountains. Making their way steadily through washes and gullies throughout the night they manage to escape detection.

As the sun rises from the west, they look out over a ridge and see a small fortress of earthen stonework blocking their movement forward. The forest is a small distance on the other side, but might as well be miles away. Everything in sight is cleared to the ground. Lights can be seen shining over the walls of the garrison and people move into and out of the gates. Looking around Ran can see patrols marching across the open terrain. Sitting down looking at the hive of activity he looks to his friends "Any ideas of how we can get passed this, the forest is so close?"

"We could walk along the edge of the hills until we find a better place to pass." Mariale thinks aloud. Looking around Balian shrugs his shoulders ,"I don't have a better idea, which way?"

"We just need to get away from here before someone stumbles on us." Ran says. Creeping over the rise to the east they slowly make their way among the low hills. Peaking over the top of the hill they stop waiting for a patrol to pass below. The soldiers are covered in mud up to their knees. The patrol wears brightly colored tabards over their heavy armor. The tabards have an image of a shield with a castle in the middle, with the sun above it. A word in a strange language is written below the sun.

Sweating in the morning sun, they wait for the patrol to pass below. The remainder of the morning is spent dodging patrols until they seem to pass into an area with less activity. Worried of being too close to the open area below they had retreated farther into the hills. Looking over at his friends Ran says, "Maybe we should go back down and see if we can pass across into the forest." Heartily agreeing they slowly move back down to the edge of the open terrain. Looking both east and west they see an area with no patrols or any garrisons in sight.

"Should we cross now or wait till nightfall?" Mariale asks them.

"We should wait till it gets dark, and then make our way across." Ran suggests. "It's only a couple hours till night." Shortly before the sun passes into the eastern mountains, a patrol passes below them moving west. Looking across the open field, Ran asks Balian. "Why is the border so heavily guarded?" Balian responds, "I don't know Ran, We need to get out of the open soon and find a safe place to rest and figure things out." Slowly leaning forward Balian looks around the boulder the three are hiding behind and looks out into the open. "What do you think, should we get going or wait till it's darker," Balian moves out a little farther seeing no one in sight. In unspoken agreement they decide not to wait.

Staying close to the ground they move out into the open, feeling as if a thousand eyes are watching them. The ground is cleared to the bare rock with nothing to hide behind. With furtive looks along the field they slowly scramble across the bare ground. Coming to the edge of the forest they see a bright light behind them opening up the sky in a stunning display of lightning.

Diving into the thickets at the edge of the forest, they look back up into the mountains watching as brilliant strokes of lightning flicker in the clouds far above. As they watch, stroke and stroke of lightning falls to the ground as if it was attacking the lower mountain sides. Great booms of thunder seem to hit them from all sides.

Looking farther down the mountainside they see bolts of lightning seemingly shoot out from the top of the hills striking the ground farther down slope. "What is that?" Ran asks. Looking around them at the forest Balian starts moving back from the edge. "I don't know Ran, but I think we should get moving. I would feel better if we put some distance between us and whatever that is!"

Moving deeper into the edge of the trees the friends look around getting their bearings. In the dark they see large round bolls of the trees disappearing into the rooftops. Long great tendrils of ivory fall down from above, like fingers reaching down to snare them. The floor farther in is clear of vegetation except small shrubs and course plants with large purple berries hanging from them. Walking up to the plants Mariale picks one, eating it before they can stop her. "What are you thinking Mariale? They could be poison!" Balian exclaims. Mariale looks at Balian with a delighted smile on her face. "I am so hungry, and they taste so good!" Looking around for more Mariale starts towards another plant. Stopping in mid stride, Mariale turns back to her friends clutching at her throat with a cry hanging on her lips.

Balian rushes to Mariale as she falls to the ground clutching her throat with her hand. Catching her before she falls to the forest floor, Balian cries her name looking into her face he holds her head with his hand. "Mariale, what have you done, Mariale!" Seeing no response Balian hugs her to his chest, a sob to his throat.

Laughing Mariale opens her eyes. "You do care Balian, running over to save me, my hero!"

"Very funny," Balian drops her to the ground turning away to hide the blush on his face. "Ouch, that hurt Balian," Mariale says as she turns over and gets up. "Good, you scared me, you little brat! That wasn't funny!" Smirking at his friends Ran looks around seeing more of the plants he starts picking berries, stuffing them in his mouth. Between mouthfuls Ran looks to his friends "Lets fill our hoods full then get out of here." They quickly gather berries for a few minutes then head deeper into the forest. "Do you two notice how quiet it is in here?" Balian asks the others. Looking around Ran notices that nothing is moving and he can't hear anything except them walking along the forest floor.

Peering through the trees Mariale moves closer to Balian, "Wouldn't you expect animals in here? Even in the cold lands at home, we see animals," she asks Balian.

"Let's find a place to wait for the morning, I don't want to stumble onto something in the dark, I think it's safer to walk during the day," Ran tells them. Moving further into the forest they find a fallen tree to hide next two. "You two get some sleep I will keep an eye out for a while."

Climbing to the top of the fallen log Ran walks along it for a few feet seeking a place to sit where he has a good vantage point. He hears his two friends move around for a minute, and then all is still underneath the trees. The quiet is almost deafening. It bothers him to the point he feels as if something out there is watching him.

Off deeper in the trees he hears a branch snap. Looking towards the noise he doesn't see anything except a low mist crawling across the ground towards them. In the corner of his eye he see's movement, but when he turns his head nothing is there. Again, he hears a branch break. Looking more intently he sees nothing but the trees and ropy vines in all directions. Feeling his hair stand on end he feels movement behind him. Starting to duck he is knocked off the log falling to the ground, his back is bruised as if a mountain came doubling down on him. Ran spits dirt out of his mouth as he rolls over trying to see what hit him. Across the log he hears his friends yelling and screaming. "Balian get away, you can't fight that!"

Hearing a loud guttural growl from across the log Ran stood up wincing with pain; to his horror as he looks towards his friends he sees a creature far taller than they with long dark bushy fur. His friends are slowly backed up against the fallen tree as it is shambling towards them with its wicked hooked claws splayed out. It is easily ten feet tall. Muscles ripple under its' skin as it moves towards them. The odor of rotten meat exudes from it, almost making him vomit from revulsion. Long hair tangled in mats covers its huge body.

With a yell Ran bounds up and over the log, as he runs toward it, the smell coming from it assaults his senses almost making him puke. When he is within twenty feet of it Ran sees Balian knocked to the ground with a swipe of the monsters arm. Mariale is on the ground screaming in terror as it readies itself for another attack.

His vision narrows as he takes all of it in a second. His senses become clearer than ever before. He smells every part of the land around him, while he instantly realizes this creature is not part of this natural forest it roams. This is the odor of a beast grown to hunt and kill. Ran sees it standing over his friends. In the flicker of an instant an image of a rune blazing in fire comes to his mind.

The creature abruptly turns, looking at Ran with bright yellow eyes. Fangs curled back into its mouth jut out of its long snout; white frothy spittle runs down its chest as it moves towards Ran. A hollow guttural scream comes from its mouth as it starts ambling towards Ran. With amazing speed it moves across the forest floor.

Without thinking Ran traces the rune in the air. Speaking an unknown word out loud, Ran points at the chest of the beast willing the energy gathered into him to flow towards it.

Mariale covers Balian with her body as she sees Ran face the creature. Not understanding why Ran is just standing there, she starts pulling at Balian to get up and run. She feels as if she is in a nightmare. Mariale sees Ran standing there pointing at the creature, trying to pull Balian away from it, she starts to yell for Ran to run when a red bolt appears in the air in front of Ran. The bolt hurtles through the dark towards the creature striking it in the chest. She hears the creature snarl in pain and rage as it momentarily halts. With another wave of Rans' hand the creature is knocked to the ground from another bolt.

All she can do is sit there on the ground stupefied with the image of her friend fighting this thing. Ran slowly approaches the creature as it lies on the ground. The nightmarish creature lies on the ground holding its chest, snarling at him. With a pitied look on his face, Ran strikes the life from it with a last red bolt of energy. Ran stands there, looking at the creature lying on the forest floor. Ran feels nothing but repulsion at ending life, even if it is evil.

Mariale jumps as Balian groans, sitting up he looks around seeing Ran standing over the creature. Smoke rises from the chest of the creature, Ran smiles at his friends. "Balian you ok? I was afraid the creature had killed you." Mariale looks Balian over, "Are you ok Balian?" Sitting up straighter Balian groans "I hurt like I was pummeled for a week at practice, but yes I can move. Are you ok Mariale?"

"I'm fine; you stopped that thing from getting to me." Ran walks over to his friends looking down at them with a sad smile he slowly sits on a log close to them. "I feel has if I fell off an ice shelf, hitting things all the way down!"

"Ran, how did you do that?" Mariale asks him. Looking around them at the forest Ran responds, "I don't know, I just saw that thing attacking you two and couldn't sit there without doing something." With wonder in her eyes Mariale looks to see how Balian is. Sitting there with a confused look on his face, Mariale stops any questions with a quick look. "I don't know if we are up to moving tonight, but we need to get out of here before another one of those things comes by, I don't know if I have the energy to fight another one." Ran stands up gingerly feeling his back where he had been hit. Balian is helped up from the ground by Mariale. His friends stand there looking at Ran expectantly holding onto each other for support. Looking back at them Ran says, "Let's just make a little distance away from here, and then we can rest. I know I need it!"

Making their way through the ever increasing mist, the forest starts growing thicker and harder to walk through, after a couple hours the three can't go any more as they almost stumble into a small bowl formed by a long rotten away tree trunk. Without the energy to fight the forest any longer they walk into the natural bowl. Each one lies down and is asleep in seconds.

The sounds of birds chirping woke Ran. The low grey light of morning surrounds them in the deep forest. Rolling over Ran sees Mariale and Balian curled up together on the other side of the bowl. Quietly Ran stands up and makes his way out of the bowl and walks a few feet away looking through the low mist creeping along the ground. Thinking about the past few days, Ran wonders which way to go. All he wanted was to get away from his home, now wondering which way to go and what to do; he doesn't hear Mariale walk up behind him.

Mariale puts a hand on his shoulder "You ok Ran?" Turning around Ran looks at her in the dim light. "I think I am, just thinking about where to go and what to do, Mariale." With a crooked grin on her face Mariale points southward, "I thought that would be obvious Ran, we need to find Britannia and fulfill your destiny."

"Yes, but which way I don't think going straight into the southern kingdom is a good idea, after all we really don't look like the people here, we need to find new clothes and figure out the land down south here, I for one have no idea where

Britannia is or how to get there"Ran replies. Balian walks up to them, "We better get going where ever there is; I heard some noise a ways back from where we came last night."

"Well, Mariale, Balian south it is until we have a better idea of where we are and where we need to go." The creeping mist of the forest envelope them as they start their way south.

Looking farther into the forest Ran see's the trees thinning and the mist slowly clearing. A branch breaks in the forest farther back; the chase has been going on all morning! Each time they think they are getting farther away from the noise in the forest it comes back closer than ever. Looking back, Ran see's movement farther back, a shadowy figure disappears behind the bowl of a tree. Looking over at Balian, Ran motions backwards and then follows his friends deeper into the southlands. For hours the three friends make their way through the trees.

They haven't seen or heard anything from behind them for hours. Stopping, Ran leans against a tree struggling for breath. "Well, what do you two think?" Mariale looks around and see's the trees thinning to the point that they can no longer hide in them. "I'm not ready for a run out in the open until we are farther away; I think we should head east from here and stay in the woods."

"I agree," Balian mutters. "We should rest abit though, my legs feel wooden." Looking around, the three friends see the forest stretching away to the right and left. To the south they see an open plain stretching away to the horizon. After a few minutes they start making their way east towards a deeper part of the trees, skirting the plain. After a little bit of time they hear horses galloping across the plain. Over a low hill a small squad of soldiers comes into view, following the tree line, though staying some distance away.

They are dressed in light clothes the color of the green and brown plains. Each one carries a spear and a bow on their back with a small sword strapped to the light saddle they ride on the horses. They hurry to hide behind trees as the soldiers gallop past them. Looking out from around the trunk of the tree, Ran see's the squad disappear over the plain and starts to rise up from the ground. From behind him he hears a grunt and feels a net cast over him. Instinctively he tries to rise and throw the net off but, finds he can't move. He hears a scream from Mariale and hears Balian grunting and trying to get out of the net that he is in.

Figures materialize out of the surrounding forest. Each of the figures is covered in green and brown clothe from head to toe, having small, sturdy bows on their backs and staves in their hands. One walks up to Balian saying something in a language Ran can't understand. The man shouts at Balian, He lifts up his stave and nocks Balian in the head ending his tussle against the net. In Rans' mind he sees the fire letters appear and imagines the net burnt away. The figures are amazed and moved away as the net holding Ran down is enveloped in fire and quickly burns away. Ran rolls away and comes to stand up, moving around to the other side of tree.

Mariale is held down by three of the men. "Ran, flee, get away from here!"

One of the men draws his bow back and fires an arrow at Ran. Quicker than the flight through the air the arrows disappears in a wisp of smoke. Ran bolts away from the tree and runs through the forest. The men in the trees grab Balian and Mariale moving back into the deeper forest. Speaking in a sweet melodic voice the leader of the men order the men to hurry and striding deeper into the forest, they disappear in seconds.

Ran makes his way swiftly into the forest not knowing what else to do. He must find his friends and rescue them from their attackers. But, until he knows who they are and how many there are he must stay alive. Ran jumps down a small hill and hides underneath a log. Ran decides to wait for nightfall and to make his way back towards where his friends were taken, hopefully discovering where they have been taken. Hunkering down among the low brush Ran waits for nightfall.

Chapter Five
The Hunters

Derhuick is getting irritated with all the noise the soldiers are making, "Why can't everyone be quite?" Looking across at Feal he motions for everyone to stop while he slips up to the top of the rise. Feal creeps up behind Derhuick, they both look over the top of the rise and see below them a land of lush green forests stretching away into the distance. But, right below them a troop of soldiers passes by on the road. They are walking quietly. After a few minutes they pass along down the road. Derhuick looks to the west and sees a small gully they should be able to crawl down and pass over the road; they need to make it to the bottom by nightfall. Derhuick motions to Feal and makes his way to the top of the gully, motioning for the soldiers to follow one at a time.

Derhuick stops at the bottom of hill at the edge of the road looking both ways, motioning for silence from the soldiers coming down the gully. Not hearing anything he hurries across the road down the hill on the opposite side taking the gully farther into the land of their ancient enemy. Farther down the mountain Derhuick see's smoke coming from the small keep protecting the northern border of the southern kingdoms. The shadows are getting longer on this side of the mountains. Derhuick looks at Feal, wondering if she will let him go after they find the three runaways. "Feal, we need to make our way farther east away from the keep if we are going to pass into the forests tonight; I don't want to wait another day up here. We are too exposed and vulnerable."

Slowly creeping out Derhuick keeps low and hurries across the road. Making it to the other side he motions for the soldiers to come across one at a time, motioning for Feal to be last.

After what seems like hours Derhuick breathes a sigh of relief after the last soldier makes it across and Feal comes up to him. Motioning down and eastward Derhuick moves to the front of the group and starts down the gully until he finds a place to leave the gully and they start across the bleak landscape moving slowly away from the keep. Scuttling from one hill to the next they travel for several hours until the sun sinks below the high peaks and shadows descend upon the southern lands.

Derhuick slowly scurried down the last ravine towards the open field looking to see if any patrols are in sight. Breathing softly Derhuick thanks his ancestors that the clouds are thick and hides the full moon approaching over the mountains. Derhuick looks up the ravine at Feal, motioning her to come down. Feal unceremoniously scrabbles down the hillside and comes to a stop next to Derhuick. Grimacing at the noise, Derhuick looks at Feal and admonishes her to be quiet. Covering his mouth he bends close to Feal and whispers close to her ear. "Feal, do you see those two trees across the field that is blackened?"

Straining to see through the darkness, Feal can just make out two gnarled trees next to a large boulder jutting out from the ground. "Next to the boulder" Feal whispers back. "Yes, Feal there." Derhuick points a little to the left, "Don't stop until you are in the edge of the forest. Now, you go first. Do not stop for anything and hide close to the edge when you get there, once you're out in the open there is no coming back! I'll follow after everyone makes it across."

Slowly Feal starts across in almost a half crawl, half run. The few minutes it takes to get across seem to last for hours, but Derhuick can see finally that she is across and into the edge of the forest. Motioning for two soldiers at a time, Derhuick starts sending the soldiers across. When the last two soldiers get ready to go, Derhuick quickly motions them to drop to the ground and stay motionless. Coming up from the west is a troop of Melcaren soldiers on horseback. Dropping back into the ravine Derhuick lies against the wall covering himself with his cloak. Slowly, the soldiers ride past them, barely looking around. Before Derhuick can say, anything both of the soldiers gets up and starts making his way across the open field.

Derhuick curses his luck. He silently follows the soldier, staying to their right. In his lowland cloak, Derhuick is silent and invisible in the dark pitch-black night. He wishes he had time to tell the soldiers how the patrols worked down here. Derhuick slowly slides his dagger out of its sheath without a sound, knowing what's coming. In the corner of his eye he sees a shadow move, a spot darker than the rest of the blackness and grips his dagger hard, ready to spring. Derhuick can just make out a shadow moving swiftly towards the two soldiers and silently curses his luck again. In the dark, he hears one of the soldiers gasp. Quickly coming up behind the shadow Derhuick grabs the back of him and plunges his dagger into the center of the shape. He feels the shadow stiffen and with a quick twist of his dagger, the fight is over. Looking over to his right Derhuick motions for the last soldier to pick up his comrade and follow him.

Derhuick heaves the lifeless body over his shoulder and quickens his pace across the open field. Coming up to the trees the two figures move into the shadows of the trees. Derhuick sees the soldiers and Feal hiding among the trees and he motions to a couple of them to take his burden. Looking back across the field, Derhuick knows they have precious moments to make some distance before the man he killed is missed. Quickly he leads them into the trees taking a path he has followed many times. After traveling through the trees for a few hundred yards, Derhuick stops by the side of the path and motions for the soldiers to stop.

"Now listen to me northerners, I know the southern lands and you don't! Do not do anything unless I tell you to, or it will most likely be your last move. Do not eat anything unless I say it is good. If we are stopped by anyone, I do the talking and no one else speaks, no matter what. Does everyone understand?" gathered around him the soldiers grunt and Feal moves to the front. "Alright Derhuick, where do we go from here, what is your plan?"

"Feal, to start with, from here on out, I am in command of this little expedition, not you! For now, we are going to hide these two and make for the middle of the forest. I have a place with clothes and weapons so we can fit in better."

Looking around the trees, Derhuick points to a large rotten log, motioning for the two bodies to be put there. Unceremoniously dropping them they soldier start pulling their shovels out. "Don't worry about covering them, the creatures of the forest will take care of that." Looking around at the group, Derhuick motions them in closer to him. "As long as we are in the forest, listen and do as I say. There are many things in here that you can't hurt. If we are separated, then head south and wait at the edge of the forest. From behind them a noise makes Derhuick look back the way they came, quickly he motions for the soldiers to line up and follow him.

At a quick walk he leads the soldiers deeper into the forest. Heading southeast, they follow a meandering path through the forest. Every so often, they stop for a few minutes while Derhuick moves out of sight scouting the trail ahead. No more sounds echo in the forest and the night moves on without incident. Derhuick notices that the light around them is getting brighter as dawn approaches. In the distant he sees an old gnarled tree. Walking up to it he looks for a small ruin scribed into the side of it. Seeing the ruin on the side he motions the soldiers to hurry. As the soldier catch up, Derhuick motions for them to wait at the tree. He moves farther ahead and seems to melt into the forest like a ghost.

Looking from one side of the path to the other Derhuick sees the stones left on the side of the path long ago. Quickly moving back to the group, he waves them forward. Following the stones to a large and twisted Oak tree, Derhuick waits for all of them to gather around. Looking around Derhuick whispers to the soldiers and Feal. "Just do what I do without thinking." Without looking back to see if they understand Derhuick jumps straight into the face of the tree and disappears. Feal looks back at the soldiers, smiling, she walks forward to the oak and jumps straight into it disappearing. Looking at each other, the soldiers grumble and curse. One by one, they each follow suite and soon the forest is empty once again.

Derhuick is standing in a pathway. Motioning each one past him deeper into the tree as they come through, "Keep moving!" he says to each of them. After they are in, Derhuick follows the passage deeper into the tree and comes into a low large circular room filled with tables and chairs. Against the far wall, a smokeless fire roars in a fireplace and the soldiers are looking around in wonder. Only Feal does not seem perturbed and is sitting by the fire trying to warm her hands. Looking up at Derhuick, she gives him a questioning look. "Well, Derhuick it seems that there are a lot of things that you haven't informed the elders of?" Looking down at here, Derhuick scowls, "Some of us prefer the warmer southlands to the bitter cold Feal, and this place has been prepared for days such as this. We need to rest after the last few days, undisturbed and hidden from Melcaren eyes."

Looking around at the group, he points to a doorway across the room. "There are beds for everyone in there and food stores enough." The soldiers come out of their daze. Some of them go into the room and throw themselves down on the beds while other just collapse at the tables looking like nothing more than bugs caught in a trap. Derhuick sits down by the fire next to Feal and smiles over at her. "Well, at least we can rest without being eaten today." Feal looks over at Derhuick with a ghastly look on her face. "What do you mean Derhuick?"

"Well, Feal, we are in the northern forest. Even the southerns do not wander through this forest in small numbers. They rarely come in here and not without large numbers. There are many creatures from the east in the forest looking for prey. I will be very surprised if those three brats make it to the southern edge!"

"Don't sell Ranwulf short Derhuick, from what I understand there is more about him then we are being told it is imperative we find him!" Getting up Feal moves closer to the fire, slowly turning around she looks at him with a serious expression. "Well, Derhuick it is time we plainly talked, you and me." Looking around Feal sees the soldiers are asleep where they sit. Looking back at Derhuick, Feal starts a pattern in the air with her hands and suddenly stops. Her mind is frozen and confused. She does not understand what is happening.

"Now, Feal you don't think I would let you use magic in one of my homes do you. This place has a protective guard around it that's prevents all magic use except mine. Yes to your question, I can and do use magic. How do you think I can pass back and forth between the northern and southern lands?" Standing up and coming close to Feal, Derhuick looks into her eyes and sees the fear in them.

"Don't bother yourself Feal. I don't like what you stand for but, I do not want to hurt you; I just do not want to be hurt by you. I promised to lead you to the boys and bring him back to the northlands. I will keep my promise." Backing away, Derhuick sits back at the table and Feal relaxes. Standing straighter Feal looks down at Derhuick and studies him for a few moments. She sees a weathered man in his late forties, care worn. Nevertheless, below his face she can see the power ebbing and flowing. She never bothered to look before. Coming out of her reverie, she asks him "How?"

Looking around the room Derhuick claps his hands and the soldiers seem to come alive. "Everyone prepare food and after we all eat, get to sleep, we have a long day ahead tomorrow." Derhuick motions for her to sit at the table with him. Coming over to the table Feal, sits down across from him. Looking at her, Derhuick looks deep into her silvery eyes. "Feal, I have traveled these lands most of my life and have learned some hard lessons, lessons that you will have to learn if you want to survive." Feal sees Derhuick shaking his head as if trying to rid himself of old nightmares.

"What lessons are you talking about Derhuick and what keeps you coming back here if it is so hard?" Feal questions him harshly. "I come back to this land Feal because of what my life as become. When I was in the northlands as a child all I remember is the bitter cold and the hard slap of my teacher. I see things have not changed much since those days. Then, one day I found a passage going deep into the castle." Catching Feal's look he responds, "Yes, Feal the same passageway we took, though I expect there are many more. I followed it until I came down out of the mountains." Standing up and taking two cups of broth from a soldiers Derhuick gives one to Feal and sips from his for a moment.

"Yes Derhuick, go on," Derhuick thinks of a life gone by and continues his story. "I wandered among the mountains for a while, not daring to come down into the forest, but eventually hunger and loneliness drove me into the forest. I remember the stories I learned about the southern people and dared not go near them, for fear they would kill me on sight. I knew I couldn't hide among them as I didn't understand them and looked nothing like them." Pacing in front of the fire Derhuick thought for a moment and then continued.

"You see Feal after a longtime of living in the forest, I came to be known as the ghost of the forest, for my skin was almost white and I learned how to move fast and silent among the trees. That was before a small group of nomads that live inside the forest caught me. They are outcasts from our kingdom and hide amongst the trees to survive. They befriended me and taught me the southern language and how to move among them as if I belonged there."

Looking at Derhuick with new respect, she wonders how long he had been living here. "How long have you been living here Derhuick, and why"

Shrugging his shoulders Derhuick answers, "I'm not totally sure but it is close to 45 years, and I live in the south because I like it and the stories we have been taught are false. The southerns do not hate us in a true sense of the word, most of them only know of us as legend. We are the race that exiled ourselves instead of learning to live amongst everyone." Finishing his broth Derhuick looks around and sits on a chair next to Feal; looking at the fire he slowly speaks his mind.

"Feal, I know what you have learned and what you teach and stand for. If you are going to complete your mission and find this boy, you must put all your assumptions behind you and look at this land with an open mind. The southern kingdoms are know what we are capable of and are fearful of that. None of them can use magic, but they make up for that in the numbers. Their armies are massive and they wage constant warfare on creatures from the wilderness in the east, and they are in constant war with the southern kingdom. In fact they built a massive wall to keep the southern kingdom from invading their lands."

Looking at Feal closely as Derhuick continues. "Also, they have a legend about our people."

"What legend is that Derhuick?" Feal asks him.

"Well Feal, the legend is called the return of the golden one. It is about a Weldon coming down and claiming a kingship over the southern lands. They will stop at nothing to prevent that from happening! Any northern that is seen in the south is chased down until caught." Derhuick tells her. "What do you mean Derhuick, hunted down and caught? And what do they do, Kill them?" Standing up Derhuick looks at Feal answering. "No Feal, they don't kill them, they do something worse. They release them into the eastern wilderness and let the creatures there take care of the problem. That will happen to us if we are caught and will happen to the three missing youths if they are caught."

Shivering Feal looks at Derhuick. "What are your plans from here Derhuick?"

"For starters, we are going to rest for a day or two and let our trail go cold that we left at the edge of the forest. Getting killed trying to find them will not do anyone any good! Get some sleep Feal and in the morning we will talk some more and figure out the best way to find them before others do." Derhuick gets up and moves into a room off to the side of the fireplace leaving her to contemplate what he had told her. After a few minutes Feal goes back to the outer room and lies down, sleep slowly enveloping her.

Nightmare images haunt her dream all night and after some time she shakes herself awake unable to bear the dreams any longer. In the main room, she hears movement and sees lights being un-shuttered. It must be morning she thinks. Getting up and coming into the main room Feal see's Derhuick settling down for a meal by the fireplace and she walks over to join him. A soldier puts some sort of gruel and drink in front of her. Shaking sleep from her eyes Feal starts eating the strange food. After a few sips of the drink, she starts to wake and quickly finishes her breakfast. She feels eyes on her and looks up to see Derhuick staring at her. She scowls at him.

"What are you looking at Derhuick?" Still staring Derhuick replies, "Just thinking…with a little tan you will fit in well down here. We must do something with your eyes though; no one here has silver colored eyes. Come with me and I will give you clothes better suited to the warm south lands." Getting up Derhuick leads Feal into his room and opens a chest piled with clothes.

"What's this Derhuick, men's clothes?" Feal starts looking through the chest trying to see everything in it. She finds pants, shirts, and scarves, but no dresses. "Is this a joke Derhuick, I can't wear pants it's not right, not proper!"

Chuckling to himself, Derhuick looks over her shoulders and points to a pair of pants and shirt and scarf. "Remember what I said last night Feal, you will have to get used to a lot of different ways down here in the south both women and men wear pants, no dresses. You will have to learn to carry a weapon too, and use it good. Get dressed and meet me in the main room. There are boots in the closet, find a tight fitting pair and bring them too."

Grumbling to herself, she changes. Feeling odd, dressed like a man, she walks back out front and moves to the table by the fireplace. Looking up Derhuick is wearing a light brown outfit with shades of light green woven into the design. He walks around to the other side of the table where it is darker and to her' amazement the clothes turn a darker shade of brown and green as if they are alive. Derhuick smiles at her. "See, this is the first step, the best way to get through the forest alive is not being seen. Now, let me see the scarf."

Feal hands the scarf over and Derhuick walks behind Feal and wraps it around her head in a complicated pattern. "That Feal the pattern worn by the woman of the southern kingdom of delamir, It tells everyone you are married and from a southern city without saying a word. I will wear the second part of the scarf. That way when we meet anyone they know right away not to question you."

Feal, looks at Derhuick and laughs hard. "You mean we are supposed to be married, Derhuick!"

Scowling at her Derhuick bites back, "Yeah, don't let it go to your head!" Quickly looking away she stifles a laugh, "Don't worry I won't." Looking around the room Feal sees that all the soldiers are dressed in the same type of clothes. What amazes her is they do not clink as they walk. She questions Derhuick about this with a glance.

"Well, Feal in order to not be seen you can't be heard so anything that makes noise must be left here. We are going to be going into the wilds in the morning." Seeing the common sense in that, Feal does not say anything else and sits down at the table fitting her puts on. To her amazement it does not seem like she as anything on, the boots fit so well and are so light.

"Alright everyone, get plenty of rest today, as we have a long way to go tomorrow and may not get a chance to rest for days to come." Looking already whipped the soldiers move back into the outer room and lay down to sleep.

Looking at Feal, Derhuick sits down across from her, "It's time for us to talk and plan this little escapade out between us, this way if I fall or you do then one of us can lead."

Chapter Six
The Journey South

All night Ranlay underneath the log with the mist closing in and silently creeping past. Every so often, he could hear branches breaking and cries of surprise cut short in the distance. Only once during the long night did Ran think he was in serious trouble, but the inky black shadow moved past him without stopping. He could feel the warmth leach out of his bones as it moved past him no farther than a few feet away. By the time, the morning rays starting coming through the treetops he thought he was going to jump out of his skin. He silently prayed to his ancestors when he felt the warmth come back into him. Slowly getting up from the damp ground Ran stretches feeling bruised and battered from yesterday.

It was all coming back to him now, the fight with the strangers in the forest and his mad run to safety. However, at what cost? Balian and Mariale taken, the first thing he had to do was find them. Looking around the forest he made his way in the direction he thought was the way he had come last night. Walking quietly through the underbrush he made his way deeper into the forest.

Looking around closer at the trees, he noticed this was an ancient forest. There were smaller trees mixed in but the older trees were massive and gnarled. With great growths of moss growing on them, He felt at home here, among the great forest. In the branches, he saw and heard a great many birds calling and chirping to each other. The deeper he went in, the closer they got. Soon it was clearer underfoot and easier going. However, looking back he saw he was leaving a clean, broad trail behind him. Well, he thought, nothing can be done about that. Walking up to a tree, he caught a glimpse of something. Bending down underneath the ferns growing at its base a piece of net was lying. "Now, at least I have a starting point," he mutters to himself. Looking Around he does not see any footprints or marks on the ground. He starts looking farther away from the tree and sees a broken fern. Looking closer he sees a small spot of blood. A few feet away he spots some light prints in the forest floor. Following the spots he starts on the trail of what he hopes is his friends. After what seemed like hours, the tracks lead right up to a tree and just stop. Ran looks around and does not see any prints going anywhere from there. Walking around the side of the tree he looking around in the area and doesn't see anything. "Now what?" he thinks to himself.

Walking back to the tree Ran finds the footprints again. "What happened, they just stop," he mutters to no one. Looking around he sees nothing to tell him where his friends have gone. Tired and lost he decides to sit down and rest for a while. He heaves himself to the ground and leans back against the tree, but he keeps leaning as if the tree was made of air.

Hands roughly grab hold of him and pull him farther backwards. His arms are violently yanked behind his back and viciously tied! The world plunges into darkness as he is blindfolded. Strong hands lift him off the ground. The last thing he hears before the world goes dark is a melodic voice in a strange language.

The soft musical voices cut through the fog as he lays bound and hooded. His arms hurt from the way he is bound and the side of his head feels tender. He wonders how long he's been unconscious. He can hear voices talking a few feet away, though it's in another language. Somewhere in the back of his mind it's familiar. Not daring to move he just tries to stay still, pain in his back makes him twitch in pain. The last thing he remembers is a shrill call before he is struck once more and darkness overtakes him.

Ran feels the rough forest floor underneath him as he comes to. He hears a scuffling noise just a few feet away and feels his leg being bumped. A slight jerk on his foot brings him fully awake. Something has got hold of his foot, jerking it. Ran slowly opens his eyes. What he sees doesn't worry him, just kind of odd. Next to his foot is what looks like a big ball of fur. Ran slowly raises himself onto his elbows, looking at the creature. Two small eyes look out at him through thick fur. A small long tongue darts out at his foot. Instinctively Ran pulls back, making the creature scurry backwards. Ran gingerly gets to his feet wondering what happened. The last thing he remembers is darkness. It looks like it is early morning by the light.

Ran hears a branch break a little distance away. Footfalls approach, through the underbrush towards him. Looking around, seeing nowhere to go, he waits behind a tree. He hears a voice call his name "Ran." Coming through the trees is Mariale and Balian. "Mariale, Balian!" Ran yells, running up to his friends he grabs them both in a hug. "What's going on, how did you get away?" Ran asks them. Looking at her friend in the morning light Mariale takes Ran by the hand and leads him over to a small clearing among the trees. Balian walks up to Ran, putting his hand lightly on his shoulder.

Looking up at his two friends Ran asks them. "What is going on, how did you get away?" Looking around them Mariale pulls at Ran's hand, "We have to start heading south Ran." Mariale tells him. Ran pulls his hand out of Mariale's grasp. "What are you talking about and what happened to you two?" Mariale and Balian look at each other. "Ran, we were taken by a group of Weldons that were outcast from our people, they have been here for years." Balian nudges Mariale. "Mariale, we must get going." Balian persists. "Well, then where are they and why don't they show themselves?" Ran asks.

Grabbing at Rans' hand Mariale pulls at him. "We have to get going, the council has sent hunters south after us, we need to get away from here. They are watching them, trying to lead them away from us." Mariale pulls once again at Ran, finally relenting the three friends start heading south among the forest. The trees start thinning abit making travelling easier. Throughout the morning, they see no one. Coming through a small copse of trees Ran is amazed to see the world open in front of them. The trees end opening onto a flat plain as far as they can see, near the horizon they can just make out mountains. Short grass the color of light green to brown grows lightly out of the ground. Already, they can see the heat shimmering in waves off of the ground. Instinctively, the three stumble backwards into the trees. Looking out over the plains, Ran looks to Mariale. "How are we going to travel over that without getting caught?" He asks them.

Mariale points to the right. "The Weldons told to head west when we got the plains Ran." Mariale tells him. Out in the distance they can see movement on the plain. Waiting a few minutes they can see a column of men on horseback galloping across the plain in the distance. "What's west of here Mariale?" Ran asks. Moving back into the trees a little distance they sit down, Balian pulls some food out of his pack that was given to them by the nomads. The three hurriedly eat while they talk. "We were told to follow the forest west until we came to the water; the only safe place in the south is an island out over the water." Mariale told him through mouthfuls of jerky.

Getting up Balian points to the south over the plains, "Look, we need to get out of here. The soldiers are coming back."

Out over the plains they see the column is slowly heading straight in their direction. If by chance or design the leader of the soldiers is bringing the Melcaren troop straight at them. Hurriedly getting up the three, move back into the forest a little distance and start heading west. "Do you think they know we are here?" Ran ponders. Looking back over his shoulder Balian starts walking quicker. The light is starting to lessen. "I don't know if they know we are here, but we need to find a place for the night." Mariale tells them. "The nomads told us to hide at night when we are in the forest; there are a lot of creatures from the eastern wilderness that are coming back into the lands now. I don't want to run into anything else!"

"Let's make some distance before night though," Ran says. Farther back from where they came, they can here sounds of metal clanking and the whinny of horses. The light is fading quickly as they come through the trees into a small clearing. On the other side of the clearing the forest is thick and close. They hurry across the open and make it into the dense underbrush. They can't see farther than a few feet in any direction. "Well, I think this is probably the best we can do tonight." Ran says in a whisper. "We should be far enough away from the soldiers not to be found tonight."

Throughout the night they take turns keeping watch, strange sounds can be heard every so often coming from the forest around them. Once, Ran is sitting there watching and sees a pair of red eyes looking at him from the trees, but when he stands up ready to shout, they disappear. Ran is still looking around when the morning light starts creeping down to the forest floor. Walking over to his two friends he nudges them on the shoulders. "Come on, it's getting light, we need to get going." Ran tells them. Waking up and getting to their feet Balian and Mariale groan and stretch. Looking round at the forest the three feel small and lonely. "Let's head closer to the edge so we can make some distance today, I feel the need to put miles between us and those soldiers." Ran tells them. Balian looks back into the forest, "I wholeheartedly agree with you, we have a long way to go and need to get across the water somehow," Balian says.

With the light growing brighter through the trees they set out. Slowly they zigzag through the trees heading slightly south until the walking becomes easier. Once in the morning they come across a small stream and drink their full while filling up their water pouches. Not wanting to stop they eat as they walk. The next few days and nights are much the same. Every so often they have to skirt a small house on the edge of the forest, and hide from Melcaren patrols. Five days from coming down to the edge of the forest they are plodding along through the trees and find a small river crossing there path.

Looking up and down stream they see no one in sight. Farther down Ran sees a row of boulders crossing the river. "Lets' make for those and cross there." He says pointing at them. Walking down the bankunder the edge of the trees they come up to the boulders. Ran a gingerly jumps onto the first one, then jumps from one to the other, following him, they quickly make it across the river. In the distance behind them, they hear a branch break. They hurry out of the open and hide in the underbrush of the forest. Ran slowly crawls back to the edge of the river looking back across.

Coming down the edge of the river, Ran sees a small group of Melcaren soldiers. The leader is dressed in chainmail from head to foot with a blue and gold tabard hung over his shoulders. On it is an eagle flying over the image of the sun. Hanging from his hip is a small sword, slung across his back is a wooden shield. Looking down at the ground, he points at their foot prints. "They went this way." He points to two soldiers' motioning for them to stay. The leader picks half of the group "you four, head back up river and make sure they didn't double back on us. The rest of you come with me, we must find them." Within seconds the men are gone, just left with two standing across the river.

Silently Ran creeps back into the forest, whispering he tells the others what he say and they slowly creep deeper into the forest away from the soldiers. None of them talk while they hurriedly make their way farther west for the next couple of hours. Finally Mariale breaks the silence saying what's on all their minds. "That was close, just a minute or two we would have been caught, we have to get out of the forest and find the water."

They travel the rest of the day going slowly through the ever increasing dense forest. The ground is getting more hilly and harder to travel. They notice it is getting hotter and wetter under the trees. They slither and slip up and down hills. Mariale feels a slight breeze on her brow. In front of them the forest goes steeply up a hill. The slowly ascend the hill noticing the forest is getting less dense as they go up and the light is getting stronger. As the trees start spreading out, they see the clear blue sky through the tops of the trees. By the time the three reach the edge of the trees they are winded and gasping for breath. The heat and air is getting oppressive they farther they travel west, making it more difficult to breath. Standing there in the edge of the trees, they see a clearing at the top of the hill. No one is in sight, as Ran puts his finger to his lips motioning for his friends to be quiet.

He motions for Mariale and Balian to stay and he points to the other side of the hill. Slowly Ran walks around the edge of the trees making his way around the side of the hill. As he comes around the other side he stops in his tracks. Looking through the thinning trees he a strange sight meets him. The land opens up out into an ocean of water. Stunned, Ran doesn't hear Mariale and Balian walk up behind him until he hears their gasp of surprise. "I never knew it would look like that." Mariale says. Coming out of his shock Ran pulls his eyes away and makes his way to the crown of the hill followed by his friends.

They stand there looking out over the ocean, in the distance all they see is an open ocean of dark water. White frothy waves spread out over it. "So, that's the water the nomads were talking about." Mariale says. Scanning the horizon as far as he can see, Ran can just make out a dark smudge on the horizon. Pointing towards it he asks his friends. "Is that where we are supposed to go, how can we possibly cross it?"

"Well, we have to cross it somehow Ran." Balian says. The three friends silently stand there and study the ocean for a few minutes. Mariale looks down the hill. "First, you two let's get to the water and see what we can find." Not wanting to leave the slight breeze of the ocean, they slowly make their way back into the deep underbrush of the forest, following a small trail west. Throughout the day they follow trails when they can steadily heading towards the ocean. Every so often they can make out the ocean as they crest a tall hill. In the late afternoon, they are following a small game trail and up ahead they can hear the muffled sound of voices. "Do either of you two have any suggestions once we get to the water?" Balian asks them. "We are obviously going to have to figure out something, we have enemies all around," Balian continues.

They can hear the voices coming closer through the trees. Looking around, Ran sees a dense cluster of trees just north of them. The head into the undergrowth, moving a few feet into the brush, they flatten out on the ground, hoping they haven't left a plain trail and are hidden. After a few minutes, five Melcarens come into view. "Well, Antonius where do we go to from here?" asks the soldier in the back. The figure in the lead stops, looking back at the soldier, "You do realize that your constant belly aching is getting very tiresome, Beler. We will keep looking for them until we find them, now shut up and keep your eyes open."

The three exchange quick glance, wondering why they are being hunted so closely. The soldiers slowly move off south. After a few minutes, they creep back out onto the game trail. Ran in the direction the soldier went, Ran comments "Well, we need to get to the water and figure out a way across, before we get caught." Following the small trail they make their way through the forest. Soon, they can hear birds in the distance; the breeze is steadily coming through the trees. They can smell the salty tang of the ocean breeze. Small glimpses of the ocean can beseen through the trees. Suddenly without warning they break through the dense forest onto the beach. They stand there for a few minutes looking around; the wind off the water is salty and cold. Small white caps break on the shore, over the horizon, the friends see it is getting late in the day, as the sun is getting low in the sky.

Looking up and down the shore Ran points south. "Let's follow the coast and see what we can find." Ran says as he starts walking along the tree line. Mariale and Balian look at each other as they follow him. The shore is fairly clear as they walk south, the trees stopping a few feet from the waters' edge. They walk for some time before in the distance they can make out smoke floating away over the water. They stop knowing that it is probably soldiers. "Well, what do we do Ran, we can't walk over the water and there is nothing north of us, if we go south we will run into soldiers?" Mariale asks him. Looking south, Ran responds. "Let's see if we can skirt past them or find a way to cross the water."

Trying to stay as quiet as possible and staying to the shadows of the trees they slowly wind their way towards the smoke. After some time, they can hear voices in the distance. Putting his finger over his lips Ran motions for his friends to follow him as he creeps forward through the trees. The voices are getting louder as they approach. Finally they can make out the voices. "How long we are going to be stuck here in the wilderness, do you think," one voice asks. The other voice responds curtly. "I don't know Beler, I'm sick of hearing your whinny voice, we were told to find the trespassers and that's that! I know better than to question my orders."

Slowly the two voices fade away as they stop to listen to them. "Well, we know it is soldiers up ahead." Ran whispers. They start slowly making their way back towards the shore. The waves rhythmically wash upon the shore as they step out from the trees. Looking up and down the shore, Ran ponders on what to do. "We know we have to make it over the water, I wonder why the soldiers are here and not back in the forest looking for us?" With a quick thought Ran tells his friends, "Wait here and I'm going to have a closer look." Before his friends can object Ran hurries away towards the south. After a couple hundred yards he walks back into the forest. He heads towards where he thinks the soldiers are camped. Winding his way through the trees for some distance, he can make out the sounds of the camp and slows to a crawl. He drops to his knees, trying to stay hidden in the underbrush.

He's close enough to the Melcarens he can make out the smells of food cooking reminding himself of his own hunger. A little ways off he can make out the sounds of people talking and slowly creeps closer. After crawling for what seems like forever, he makes it to the edge of a great clearing. Peeking out from among the trees he sees a clearing made by the soldiers across a bay of water. Tents are spread out in single rows, maybe ten in all, with campfires among them. Melcaren soldiers are spread around the open bay, tending to their armor or eating. Ran sees twenty or so small groups of them scattered around. What draw his interest are the fifty small boats pulled up to the shore. He waits and watches awhile. He's' close enough he doesn't dare move any more than he has. The soldiers slowly break up into smaller groups as the light begins to fade. They stoke the fires higher and Ran takes his chance to creep back into the forest. Slowly making his way back to his friends, Ran tells them what he found, and he starts to form a desperate plan.

"Mariale, Balian, We need one of those boats to get away from here and over the water," Ran tells them. Looking at Balian Mariale asks Ran, "What is your plan?"

"I will lead you two back to the boats and then after I make a commotion, I will lead the soldiers away. When they come after me, take one of the boats. Bring it back here and I will find you," Ran explains. Mariale answers, "Are you mad Ran? You'll get caught."

"Not if I'm fast and you get back here to get me, we need a boat to get away. The south is closed to us now and there nothing back where we came from. We must make it across the water. Let's go before it gets any later."

Without a better option, they slowly make their way back to the bay. Peeking out from the trees they see the camp is quiet. A few guards are sitting around the fires, while the rest of the soldiers sleep. Ran points to the boats and motions to his friends to wait. Creeping away from them Ran slowly makes it to the other side of the bay without alerting the camp. When he is on the other side of the camp he cautiously creeps back to the edge of the clearing. Looking out from the trees he sees everything is still quiet. He slowly stands up; in his minds' eye he forms a pattern of fire. Looking out over the camp he picks a fire in the middle and imagines a fireball hurtling towards it. Before he realizes it a large ball of fire shoots from his outstretched hand, quicker than he can see, it speeds' past the tents and envelopes the fire. He hears a thunderclap and the fire explodes. Soldiers jump up in fright, yelling and screaming. The camp is in turmoil, as Ran flings another one at another fire. Soldiers are flung to the ground by the concussion of the explosion. Soldiers are pouring out of their tents pulling on their armor and weapons. A few point towards his direction yelling and screaming. Without looking back Ran turns and flees from the assault on the camp, knowing they will be after him in seconds. The leader quickly musters his soldiers into a line across the edge of the trees and they start the chase after him. Ran can hear shouts and screams of the wounded and dying as he flees in a large circle back towards the north.

Across the bay, Mariale and Balian lay and watch the chaos in the camp. They are stunned once again as they see two fireballs envelope fires in the middle of the camp. Shaking her head, Mariale smacks Balian on the shoulders as the last soldier disappears into the forest. Quickly, they get up and run to one of the boats. Mariale jumps in grabbing an oar as Balian pushes it out into the water, then jumps in. grabbing the other oar; they row out of the bay into the dark open water. They slowly make their way back up the shore towards the meeting spot. They can hear in the distance the sound of explosions and yelling and screaming as the Melcarens pursue Ran.

Coming up to the shore, Mariale and Balian quickly turn the boat around, waiting for Ran to appear. The yelling and screaming is getting closer as they sit and wait. From inside the forest they hear one more explosion beforeRan pelts from the forest edge. Streaming out from behind him are soldiers intent on capturing him. "Go!" yells Ran at the top of his lungs. Balian quickly pushes the boat out from the shore as Ran jumps into it and grabs an oar. Furiously they paddle away from the shore. Mariale sitting in the front watching Ran in amazement.

On the shore the soldiers are gathered, while some are running back to the camp to get to the boats and follow. The leader stands at the shoreline silently looking at them. The three make their way out into the open ocean in the dead of night, not knowing what to expect. Leaving the sounds of the Melcarens behind them, the noise slowly fades away until they hear nothing but the waves slapping against the side of the small boat.

Throughout the remainder of the night, they take turns rowing. In the distance the light of the camp steadily grows dim until it winks out over the horizon. The three friends look at each other wondering what is the future is going to hold. Slowly the light starts to grow over the horizon as they silently row, each one deep in thought. Ran, in the front looks ahead of them and out in the distance he can see the smudge has become a set of great cliffs running down to a great rocky shoreline. Exhausted they stop rowing and stare at the cliffs miles ahead.

"Somehow he has to get over those and see what we can find." Ran tells them. The morning light breaks across the horizon and looking back they can't see any sign of pursuit. They take turns rowing throughout the day as one of them sleeps in the front. It is cold and winding out in the open water. By the middle of the morning they are all soaked and chilled to the bone. Fitfully sleeping when they can, suddenly the boat is caught in a current and try as they might they can't break away from it. They are being drawn straight into the rocks on the shore. Finally when they are within a few hundred yards of the shore they give up on trying to row away and hold on to the sides of the small craft. As they come closer to the shore the waves break over the top of the boat drenching them more, the boat is filling up with water foundering.

Suddenly a strong wave crashes up against the boat and flips it over. The three are flung out into the water as they struggle for breath in the crashing wave. Balian is thrown up against a rock crying out in pain, and then is quickly washed back into the water. The current grabs them and pulls them towards the shore. After sometime fighting the waves, they find ground under their feet and limp ashore onto the cold grey rock of the beach.

Great grey cliffs loom over them as they collapse on the beach, cold and battered. Balian lays there groaning in pain. After a few minutes Ran finds the strength to stand and makes his way over to Mariale and Balian, seeing Balians face grey pain. He kneels down beside him. Looking at his friend he sees his shirt is bloody. Pulling it up, he sees a great black bruise spreading across his side, with blood welling up around a small cut. Mariale kneels next to Balian cradling his head in her lap. Looking around Ran sees nothing but the overhanging cliffs. "Can you stand Balian?' Ran asks him. Grimacing in pain, Balian comes to his feet with his friends help. "Yeah, I can stand though I don't think I can walk fast."

Mariale grips Balian around the shoulders and he takes a few tentative steps. "I can walk, definitely away from here. This cold lonely place makes me feel trapped." He says. Ran lets go of his friend and looks up and down the beach, searching for a way to get up and over the cliffs. All he sees is more cliffs and rocky beach. "Well, I guess going one way is just as good as the other, I would like to be up on the cliffs by nightfall." Ran tells them. Looking south along the shore Ran sees a small worn trail meandering among the rocks. "What's that he wonders" to himself. Ran walks closer to it and sees signs of footprints in the rough grainy sand. He looks back to his friends "Hey, I think I found a trail!" he shouts. With a few steps Ran notices Balian starts to walk a little more normal, not hunching so much to his wounded side. "Balian, if you feel like you need to stop and rest, say something." Ran can hear Mariale admonishing him.

For the next couple hours they stumble and climb over the rocky beach, finally by the middle of the morning they are starting to dry out from the water. The path they found meanders up and down the beach steadily going south. With a quick turn towards the cliffs it ends in a gaping hole leading away into the base of the cliff. Coming up to the entranceRan looks around seeing nowhere else he proceeds into the gaping maws of the cliff. Walking a few feet he stops waiting for his eyes to adjust to the sudden darkness. He can just make out a staircase ahead. It's warmer inside out of the wind. Thinking of his hiding place what seems so long ago, he silently makes as ball of pure white light appear in his hand. The cave walls extend for yards above them with a small steep staircase roughly cut out of the cliff going up. Moisture glistens on the walls. "Do you need to rest before we head up Balian?' Ran asks him.

"For just a few minutes, my side is hurting but we need to get up there." Balian says as Mariale helps him sit down. "Ran, what do we do once we get up there?" Mariale asks him. Looking back at his friends, feeling responsible for them being here, he responds. "I'm not sure Mariale; I know first we need to get help for Balian." He says as he looks around the empty cave. "Who do you think made this staircase?' He says. Looking up, Balian says. "I couldn't imagine, but I for one am glad it's here. How else could you get up the cliffs?"

Balian groans as he gets to his feet, catching Mariales eye he says. "I can rest on the way up if I need to, let's go." Helping

Balian, Mariale helps him climb the stairs, Ran taking the lead. For what seemed like hours, the three climbed the stairs, stopping for brief rests. They feel a slight breeze from up above and start seeing a light glimmering farther up the stairs. Ran motions for his friends to stay and creeps up the stairs to see what's ahead. Coming back in a few moments, he motions his friends to follow him. "We are almost to the top, I don't see anyone about."

Slowly they follow the steps up to the top coming out in the bright light looking out over a plain with stunted grass. A stiff cold wind blows up over the tops of the cliffs. In the distance they can see outcroppings of rock and bare earth. Ran looks around and sees no indication of which way to go. "I suggest we go inland away from the wind and try to find a place to hide out for the night until we can find out about this place." They climb up out of the staircase, Ran looks back and is stunned his sight. Out back from where they came, he can see the outlines of a huge forest. Blending away south of it is a plain of unimaginable size. From this distance he can't make out anything in in particular. Up north he sees on the horizon the mountains where he was raised, all covered in white. Shivering to himself, he thinks of the horrors of his youth. The spell broken, he turns away looking back over the plains they are on. Slowly, they start making their way across the windy plains, heading for the rock outcroppings.

Balian sees a flicker of movement out of the corner of his eye. Looking that way he sees nothing. Just wind swept plains. Ignoring the flicker they continue on almost to the first outcropping. Ran walks up the outcropping, being only a few feet high, He leads his friends around the side of it. Coming around the edge, they see an unbroken plain. In the distance the can see smoke over the top of a hill. "Well, atleast someone lives here."Ran says. "For some reason the Melcarens didn't want us to get here, so maybe we can find friends here." Mariale continues his thought. They walk slowly towards the smoke, the plain dropping so the wind isn't so strong; warmth seems to flow into them without the biting wind at their backs. They see the sun starting to set behind the plains, it will be getting dark soon Ran thinks. From behind them they hear pebbles tumbling. Turning around they are confronted with a strange sight. Sitting on the outcropping, is a small girl of maybe ten years. She is wearing, overlarge pants and a shirt of sack cloth. What catches their eyes is the dark brown hair and silvery eyes staring back at them.

Chapter Seven
Revelations

Staring at them is a small Weldon girl. The three exchange glances. Ran approaches the outcrop that she is sitting on. Looking up at her, he doesn't quite know what to say. "I see your hunger and you are lost, that much is obvious." The girl tells them. "But first, tell me your names and I will tell you mine."

Not quite sure what to say Ran Stammers. "I'm Ran, well, Ranwulf, my friends are Balian, and Mariale. Yes, we are hungry and lost. Who are you and what are you doing here?" Ran answers her. Totally confused, he stands there gaping at her. "My name is Nellian. I live just over the hill there." She says to them and pointing back over their shoulders. "It has been awhile since I talked to my own people. Come with me." Jumping down, Nellian walks past them towards the smoke in the distance. Not knowing what else to do, they follow behind her, each looking at her. Catching up to her Ran asks her. "Um, Nellian, you said you live here?"

"Of course Ranwulf, I've been here all my life." She answers him over a sharp gust of wind. They can smell the faint smell of rain on the wind. "Let's hurry back, so I may look at your friend Balian, and we can get out of this cold."

Quickening her pace, the three are hard put to keep up, especially Balian. Soon, Mariale and Balian fall behind. Without much choice, Ran falls back and stays with his friends, wondering about this girl and who she is. Walking up and over the top of the hill they see a small one room cottage in the bottom of a little valley. A goat is tied to a stake on the side of the cottage. The three can see bright lights streaming from the windows. Smoke is rising up from a chimney in the center of the cottage. Other than a stack of wood by the door, it looks nothing more than a lonely out of the way home. The front door is open wide. They come down the hill, and stop in the doorway looking into the small house. Inside they can hear Nellian moving about the small cottage. "Come in you three and close that door." Nellian calls to them. Abashed, they walk into the cottage, closing the door behind them.

In the center of the cottage is an open fireplace, with a table on one side and small benches spread around it. Odd and ends are scattered about haphazardly. Containers of different powders and herbs are stacked everywhere.Coming over to Balian, Nellian takes him by the hand leading him over to the fire. "Sit down here and let me see where you are hurt, son." Mariale and Ran look at her, wondering who she is exactly. Nellian quickly sets a kettle on the fire and puts some herbs in it. Coming back to Balian, she pulls Balian shirt up and sucks in her breath. "Balian, you should have taken care of this hours ago, it has started to fester."

Feeling has if his mother is fussing over him; Balian looks away and grimacing as Nellian starts to clean to his wound. The kettle in the fireplace starts to whistle. Nellian looks up from her duty. "Ran, be a dear and pour each of us a cup of that." Ran quickly finds four cups by the sink and hurriedly pours four cups of the sweet smelling tea. Soon, the wind and cold are forgotten as they sip there tea and relax in the warmth of her cottage. After finishing with Balians wound, she sits back and drinks deeply from her cup.

Balian sits there in front of the fire nodding off. Looking up Nellian points to the back of the cottage. "Balian, why don't you lay down for a while until we can get some food ready." Sleepily Balian makes his way back to a cot and quickly falls asleep. "Nellian, who are you and what are you doing here on this cold land." Ran asks her. Feeling exhausted and sleepy

Mariale goes back to Balian and is soon asleep next to him. Ran looks closely at Nellian, she looks nothing more than a ten year Weldon girl, but for the fact her presence exudes peace and power. She is sitting there by the fire swinging her legs underneath the bench she is sitting on. More confused than ever Ran asks her again, "Nellian, who are you really and why are you here?"

Coming out of some sort of memory, Nellian looks up at Ran and before his eyes she shimmers, changing into a tall woman in her twenties. She has the same silvery eyes, but her hair cascades down her back in locks sprinkled with gold. She is the image of Weldon beauty. She smiles over at him, laying her pale hand on his arm. "Ranwulf, I have been waiting for you." Struck by her beauty and graceful form Ran sits quietly waiting for her to continue. "I was sent her a longtime ago, to wait for your coming into the world. Look at me Ranwulf, you have a destiny to fulfill and I am here to set you on your way."

Looking into her eyes, Ran sees long haunting memories floating in them. He feels his head swimming, but unable to tear his eyes away he seems to be falling into them. Ran looks deep into her eyes and the world slips away. Memories come flooding back from times past; he remembers his childhood and more.

Bright light is streaming through the window of our hovel, coming awake, I see my father roughly shove by my mother as he stumbles out the door. It is cold and I am hungry. Absently I flick bugs off me and a rat scurries off my bed as I sit up. In the light, I see tears streaming down my mum's face before she turns around. I have seen that enough times in my ten years to know that my dad is mad again. Softly she tells me to get up and start my chores. I wince from the cold as I stand up on the dirt floor, wishing once again for something to cover my feet with, but we are poor and do not have things like shoes.

The only light and warmth we get is from the rush we grow for light at night.

As I go outside, I can see my father standing by the well getting sick. I know from the past to stay away from him for most of the day. He gets mean sometimes after he comes home late after going into town. My back still hurts from the last time I spilled the goat's milk I was getting for mum. Hurrying, I run around the back of the hovel to start milking Rulf the goat for breakfast. I named her Rulf after my dog, my father took him away because I brought him inside one day and he stole a chicken from the pen. Quickly I fetched the pail hung on the wall and started milking old Rulf. A lot of the time, I sit next to her and talk to her while she looks at me as if I am a fool. However, today she is prancing around and looking at me with wide terrified eyes. I can barely get her to stand still long enough to milk her. Finally, I get a pail full and start back around the side of the shack. Right before I get to the corner I feel the hairs on my neck stand up, like when lightning strikes really close. I stop walking when I hear voices out front.

Slowly I creep up to the edge of the wall and peek around the corner. I can see my sire talking to someone. I cannot see whom he is talking to, so I creep a little farther around the edge. The sight of the cloaked figure freezes me. A cloak covers it so much I cannot make out anything, except the sword hanging off its back. I cannot help but look at the horse; it is covered in big plates of black metal, from the mouth all the way back to the tail. The figure on the horse makes me shiver and shake where I kneel! I see my father slowly reach out and take a small bag from the figure and it clanks when he grabs it. He motions towards the house then walks away. The figure looks up and I cannot move. Red eyes peer out from under the cloak and transfix me with their stare. As if in a nightmare, the figure on the horse comes up to me, reaches down grabbing me by the neck, and lifts me over the horse in front of it. Inside the house, I hear mum crying and sobbing. That is the last time I see the little shack on the hill, my last memory of home is bumping up and down on the horse with my mum looking out the window staring after me.

I feel that cold bony hand clamped around my back while I am bumping up and down in the sunny cold day. My ribs feel as if they are bruised and broken, after hours of jostling up and down hills and mountains the horses pace quickens and I see a road coming up that goes straight up the side of a mountain. Fog covers the top of the mountain. The rider on the horse clamps his hand tighter on my back. Back and forth up the road, we go, hours and hours it seems to go on. Slowly the fog surrounds us and I cannot see more than a few feet away. Everything is grey and white, except once in a while I can see shapes in the fog. Some are small, and others go by so fast, there just a blur.

After an eternity, the horse stops and I feel the rider shift around waiting for something. I try to look around and swiftly the rider cuffs me in the back of the head. I can hear movement a few feet away from me and hear a slow screech like gates moving on rusty hinges. Once again, I feel the horse is moving forward and I hear the steady clip clop of the hooves on stone. Slowly the fog is giving way and I peek out from closed eyes to see faint torch light and a grey cobbled stone road underneath the horse. I feel the horse stop and the world goes black again when a bag the thrust over my head. The figure grabs me roughly and jumps off the horse, carrying me like a sack of grain. I can hear his footfalls hitting the stone, like doom marching down the road. Then, He roughly drops me onto the cold floor and I hear a low grating voice next to my ear telling me not to move.

"What's your name boy?" A deep voice asked me. I stammer, "Ranwulf." In the distance I hear a bell tolling and I hear movement in the room, then all is quite. I can hear a door open and boot falls come toward me. Hands roughly jerk me up and I feel a cold bony hand grab the sack over my head forcing my head back. I can vaguely see shapes through the cloth pressed against my eyes. The cloth is forced up over my lips and I feel hot burning liquid poured down my throat.

"You better be right about this, Melcore!" a voice says. "My lord, He is the very one that we have been looking for! That is without doubt." "Not in front of the boy, Melcore. We have to make sure he makes it past the change first." I remember nothing else, as black envelopes me. Blackness overtook me and I remembered nothing for a time. Waking up, I found myself lying in a soft bed with people around me. Sitting on the bed next to me peering intently at me was an old man in a blue robe, with wispy grey hair floating above his head, "Are you back with us boy?" he asked. Opening my mouth, I could only croak out barely a yes, mainly by bobbing my head up and down. The old man gingerly pats my hand "that's good son, don't try to talk, I'll be back later to check in on you, name is Orist if you need something." I could almost hear his bones creak when he leaves the room. While we were talking all the servants had disappeared and I was all alone. The first thing in my mind was my mum, strangely though, it felt like that was a lifetime ago and it did not matter anymore.

As I turn to my side, I look around the room and see heavy cloth tapestries of battles and people hanging on the walls. In the corner is a big fireplace with a shield hanging over it. On the shield are two wolves facing each other, between them are two crossed swords, being illuminated by the rising sun behind them. I feel like I have seen this picture before, but cannot remember when. Looking down, below the shield I see the figure of a person sitting in one of the chairs facing the warmth of the fireplace. The last thing I see before I fade to sleep is an arm laid across the armrest of the chair. Nevertheless, in wonder and fear I see a bony hand with long claws at the end of the fingers poking out of the sleeve. In my dreams during the night, I am running from something or someone and cannot get far enough away to escape. I am running through cold stone halls. Every time I turn around to see behind me, I catch a glimpse of a tall slender shadow just outside of the light of the torch I am holding. A long billowing dark robe drapes the figure. Two red eyes pursue me down the halls. I barely run fast enough to get away. Down one of the halls, I hear a sound of many voices talking. Fleeing in hopes of finding someone, I run towards the noise. Soon I see a light and the voices are getting louder. Now I am hearing the sound of footfalls getting close behind me. In a last burst of speed, with my ragged breath in my throat, I burst out of the doorway from the hall. I catch my foot on something and sprawl headlong into the room.

The voices in the room go quite and the light goes out in a flash. Behind me, I hear soft footfalls approaching. Not daring to look up, I lay there and wait for my death to come. The footfalls go silent and I cannot hear anything above the noise of my heart hammering in my chest. I catch my breath and feel a sob coming up; "NO" I will not let myself cry. I fearfully raise my head and in the dim shadows, I look around to see where I am. I see torches set in nooks along the walls with long stringy cobwebs hanging off them. Along the walls are shreds of long forgotten tapestries. Rotten remains of once richly decorated chairs line the walls. Rusty suits of armor stand between each chair, full of cobwebs and ages of disuse. Across the room is another door leading out of the room. Hearing rustling from behind me, I hurry across the room and look down the hallway. I see just darkness and dusty cobwebs. From ahead of me I hear voices coming towards the room. I hastily look around ducking my head, as if I am somewhere I am not supposed to be.

I creep down the hall, keeping one hand on the wall to steady myself. I feel a draft coming behind me from the room I just left. The stone hallway twists and turns with gaping dark holes every so often. Suddenly I feel air below my foot and discover a staircase going down, not wanting to go back I descend the stairs. It is getting colder and damper as I go down and find myself shivering from the cold. At the bottom of the stairs, I see the reflection of a light and slow down to a crawl. Slowly I creep the last few feet down the staircase and move towards the doorway. Peeking around the edge of the doorway, I see a room full of people, sitting on rich, deep, furniture. All of the figures are dressed in rich elegant clothing and armor. Across the room, I see a richly robed man sitting on a huge chair. Never seeing a Man like that, I am amazed. My eyes are drawn to him like seeing the light of day for the first time. He seems so familiar to me. Standing up I see his dark brown hair held by a simple golden circle. He is wearing a jeweled sword on his back and holding his hands up to everyone in the room, motioning for quiet.

He motions for a figure from the crowd to come forward. Frightened by the sight, I see the figure that took me what seems like a lifetime ago. He kneels down in front of the man by the throne. "Melcore stand, you know we are informal here." The voice I hear from the man tugs at my heart, as if I was home.

"Yes my Lord," Melcore turns around to the crowd of people, "My Lords and Ladies, I am the one that found the boy. I know from the signs that he is the one we have been seeking. It has been two days since the test, and he is still alive. He is the only one that has lived through the change!" Walking around the edge of the throne Melcore stops, throwing his cloak aside, and my breath catches in my throat as I see the most spectacular person. He has dark brown hair and fiery red eyes. Standing about six feet, he projects an aura of knowledge and power. His hair falls around his shoulders, cascading down his back like a waterfall. He wears gold and black armor intricately engraved with runes of power. Hanging from his back is a jeweled scabbard holding a beautifully gem encrusted hilt of a Long sword.

"I have searched the world for a long time to find this lad; I remember the words spoken to portend his coming into this age. He will lead us into the new age!" Melcore moves to the throne next to the lord and kneels down in front of him. "Lord Roanoled, I pledge to you with my life and the blood flowing in my veins that Ranwulf is the one we have searched for! This very day he has proven himself to us"! Swiftly standing up and pointing at me from across the room I hear his voice float across the room towards me as everyone turns and stares at me! "Behold Ranwulf, who else but the chosen one could search out and find our counsel! Only the chosen few left on this world have the power and providence to be here." I feel my head spinning. I feel pulled and I cannot get away from what I know what must come. The feeling of dislocation crushes me.

The walls become insubstantial; I see the heavens above me, the glory of the universe all around me. The walls of the castle become like wisps of smoke upon a wind. In the distance, a small bright white light approaches. Slowly, but with ever increasing speed it comes closer to me. The pure white light filling my vision blinds my eyes. Slowly the light diminishes. I feel a hand lightly touching my arm. I rise to my feet and slowly open my eyes, seeing the face of whom I know is my father. He is dressed in golden armor with a jeweled sword at his hip.

I see myself in the future, a figure of power I am destined to become. The beautiful music of harps plays just beyond my hearing, coming and going at Random. "Son, you have come to me, I have yearned for this day to come to pass." I look up at him, finally for once in my short life I feel at peace, all the worries of the past are gone.

"Ranwulf, you have been brought to us at the appointed time. Our people have wondered far upon the winds of time. It is your appointed task to learn and grow into your inheritance. When you are ready, you will realize your place in the world and lead us".

"Father!" I scream as I am pulled back to the small lonely cottage. The haunting music fades to just a memory as I feel the stone floor underneath my knees. I jolt out of my memories with tears streaming down my face. "Father, Father!" Opening my eyes I see Nellian looking into my eyes knowing she feels and shares my pain. "Yes, Ranwulf that's who you are and who you are meant to become. But, first you must find yourself and become whole again. You must find your birthright in this land." Nellian says tooRan as she holds him tight. Getting up Nellian takes Ranwulf by the hand leading him to a small bed in the back next to his friends. "Ran, sleep for now and recover your strength, we will talk in the morning." Feeling overwhelmed and confused Ranlies down. The last thing he remembers is the sweet music coming back to him before the welcoming darkness.

Waking up in the grey morning light Ran feels refreshed and alive for the first time he can remember. Rolling over he sees Mariale sitting next to Balian. She is soaking his forehead with a wet cloth. Getting up Ran walks over to Mariale, "How is he doing?" he asks sitting down on a chair next to them. "He's has a fever that won't break. The bleeding has stopped, but the wound is festering." Mariale worriedly tells him. "Nellian has gone to find herbs she says will help him."

Realizing for the first time she has left the cottage, he walks over to the window looking out. A cold grey, world waits for him out there. He knows what he must do, but doesn't know how to start. He just wants to go somewhere and be left alone to live in peace and quiet. His destiny, what does that mean to him he ponders. He must help a people out that have been cruel to him. Why? It seems that everyone wants to kill him or imprison him. The memories from last night surge into his mind. It all seems crazy right now in the cold light of day. Who was he after all, just a small person in a big world, how could anyone expect so much from him? How was he supposed to lead a culture that was so harsh and closed in upon itself? He could barely keep himself alive one day to the next. The door closing brings him out of his thoughts. Looking over he sees Nellian the small girl crossing the room to the fire place. Unceremoniously she dumps the contents of a small bag into a pot hanging in the center of the fire.

Turning around a curt movement of her head brings Ran over to her. They sit down at the table, Nellian intensely staring at his face. "You are troubled Ranwulf." It wasn't a question he thinks. "Nellian, how can I be the person everyone says I am?" He asks her. "Ranwulf, at this moment you are not that person, but you will become him when the time is right. First you must find your birthright." Looking back out the window he thinks for a minute then turns back to her. "Nellian, what exactly is my birthright, how can I find something when I don't know what or where it is?" Ran asks her.

With sympathy in her eyes Nellian answers, "Ran that I don't know. The only thing I can say is it is here on this island of Britannia. You must find it and yourself." Groaning out loud Ran looks away. "Tell me this Nellian why should I help a world that hates me. I just want them to leave me alone!" Standing up Nellian walks over to the fire, lifting the kettle from its hook. "Ranwulf, the world doesn't hate you; it is scared of what you are. Your innocent, you see the world in black and white, when it is really shades of grey like the plains outside. You live inside the light. There are many creatures and people that live in the dark." Taking the kettle Nellian wets a cloth instructing Mariale to wrap Balians wound with it.

Turning once again to Ranwulf, Nellian walks to the window looking out. "Nellian, I don't know what to do or where to start, even if I wanted to."

Chapter Eight
The Turiec

The winds cuts through their heavy furs, Heastin feels the cold bitter wind cutting through his skin like daggers. After hours of searching, they have found nothing, eventually giving up. They finally approach the tree. Stumbling down the slope to the cave, they almost fall on the floor.

Two of the scouts hurry over to help them. "Are the others back?" Heastin asks, the scout answers "No, Sir not yet." The warmth feels almost as bad as the cold. Heastin feels his skin prickling and stinging from the sudden heat. From up the slope Heastin hears footfalls coming down. Hurest stumbles down the slope dropping to the ground at the bottom. The men hurrying to help him suddenly stop before they reach him. Bringing their hands up, they stumble backwards. Heastin walks up to Hurest, looking at him, he doesn't see anything. Hurest slowly looks up and Heastin can see both his eyes are torn out. The sockets frozen solid, shocked, Heastin stops. Over the wind outside the men can hear a low rumble and growling. Spurring his men into action, Heastin shouts. "Get ready the Turiec have come." Jumping to the side of the slope Heastin pulls out his longsword. Just as he hits the wall, a white fur clad body hurtles past him, taking the man behind him instead. In seconds he is disemboweled with a rake of itssword. Whipping his longsword backwards Heastin takes the thing in the back. Barely stopping, the creature reaches back and nocks Heastin to the ground.

The creature grabs the sword, pulling it from its body. With a howl of glee, it launches itself into the middle of the stunned men. Recovering, Heastin sees two more Turiec come down the slope. Each one heedlessly launching itself into the men, picking his sword up from the ground Heastin prepares to join the fight when the world seems to freeze, even the Turiec turn towards the entrance.

The ground rumbles and pitches under their feet, throwing everyone to the ground. Before the men can react the Turiec flee back up the tunnel, disappearing into the blowing snow. Heastin quickly moves next to the tunnel entrance trying to see up it. As he looks into the blowing snow outside, it starts to slacken and then suddenly stops. Moving back to his men he surveys the dead and wounded. Looking over at Feruch, Heastin points to the badly wounded on the ground motioning to him. Quickly Feruch walks over to them and quickly silences them with a thrust of his sword. Gathering his men together Heastin tells them. "I don't know what would cause the Turiec to flee, but I would rather face it in the open. Spread out on the sides of the tunnel and let's atleast find the end with honor."

His men nod to him, spreading out they slowly make their way up the tunnel and out into the open snow field. Looking around confused, Heastin and the men see nothing. The snow has stopped. There's not even a slight gust of wind. Nothing but white as far as they can see, Miles to the south beyond the tree is the castle, looking around Heastin sees nothing but snow and ice over the fields.

Turning towards Feruch, Heastin begins to ask a question then suddenly stops. For out in the distance, he sees a shimmering white light approaching, floating over the ground. "What is that?" Heastin asks. As the light approaches, the men can start to make out a form inside the light. A tall figure slowly comes into view as the light comes closer. A figure dressed in rich white robes of middle years takes shape a few yards away. He has pale skin in contrast to his jet black hair. He stands looking at the ground, not moving. His hands hidden in folds of his robe, Heastin brings his sword up ready for an attack, not sure what to expect. At the movement the figure looks up, stunning them in place. For his eyes are golden.

Legends of old speak of a terrible power living in the northern wastelands. Heastin dares not move, feeling like a bug under the gaze of the man. Long ago it was said, when the Weldons first came to this land, they fought and overpowered a race of powerful beings. After a long and terrible battle, it was told the king banished them to the ice fields. Moving his gaze past Heastin the figure looks at the castle with a wickedly cruel smile. The spell being broken Heastin leaps towards the man. His sword outstretched in a vain attempt of attack.

To Heastin, the figure seems to move impossibly fast. In the blink of an eye, he has a long black sword in his hand. The last thought on Heastin's mind before he is sliced in twain is, how can his people fight this power? Turning to the remaining men the figure ends their lives in seconds. With blood dripping off the banefully glowing sword, the figure turns towards the north. In a terrible voice like thunder he calls aloud. "Now, my children our time is at hand at long last. Come to me!"

Out from over the plains an army of legend slowly approaches the Weldon stronghold. Turning around, the figure starts moving closer to the walls of the castle. Silently surveying the castle, the figure looks up and sees someone staring back at him. Memories of old flood back into his mind. Revenge, hate, bloodlust fills his chest. Casting his robes to the snow, the figure is resplendent in polished jet black armor intricately engraved in runes, shimmering blue in the cold white light of day. With a growl of hatred, the figure points the sword at the figure, a great white bolt of lightning flies from the sword, shattering upon an invisible wall, feet from him.

On the battlement Melcore looks down, seeing death visited upon his men on the snow. The council is silently gathered around him looking on. In horror they stand and watch the figure cut down every man in the snow in seconds. "Melcore, who is that, why don't you do something to stop him?" a council member implores.

Looking away after the slaughter, Melcore answers. "Belias that is a legend of old we see. I know its power and we can't hope to defeat it now. He is Meroth, once the king of the race that dwelled in our land."

Feeling the bolt explode upon his defense Melcore turns his attention back to the ice fields below. Looking down from the battlement, Melcore stares at Meroth. "We have not grown weak Meroth. You may not cross the border into our realm." The council members back away feeling immense power emanating from both figures.

"It has been long since I cast my eyes upon you Melcore. I feel the weakness in your people. Very soon youWeldons shall be obliterated, disappearing from this world utterly." Swiftly turning Meroth moves northward towards the approaching army, turning back towards the remaining council members, "Prepare our people for war, we have nowhere to go and must defend our home from the Turiec. We have scant hours till the first assault upon us! Belias stay. After our people are prepared the rest of you join me in my chambers."

"Belias, stay upon the battlements and at the first sign of attack send word to me." Melcore strides off the castle wall, going to prepare for the inevitable battle. The castle is a flurry of activity, as the Weldons man the walls preparing for the assault. Questions and rumors are flying faster than the winds. At best the defenses are confused and unorganized. The Weldons have not had to fight in ages. Sitting in his chambers, Melcore wonders silently how long it will take the Turiec people to break through the walls and overwhelm them. He must assure that as many Weldons as possible get away. Memories come flooding back from ages ago, memories of the Turiec ferocity. How many Weldons died fighting them? We were much stronger then, thinks Melcore. Still, His people must defend as long as they can, they will have to flee to the eastern cities in the end he knows. Silently Melcore vows to make as many Turiec pay until then.

Footsteps coming up the stairs alert him to the council's presence. Melcore moves to the other side of the room as they file into his chamber. Looking around the room, Melcore sees his peoples' only chance of survival. Tension is thick in the room; every Weldon council member knows they stand on a precipice. Melcore looks around the room, his eyes coming to rest upon Daus, the youngest of them. "Daus, you must go south and somehow find Feal. Tell her what is happening here. She must continue her mission at all costs. Tell her..." stopping and looking around at all the council he continues, "Daus, tell her most likely by the time you find her that the council is no more and our people have been dispersed to the four winds. None of us here tonight will likely survive the coming battle."

Murmurs and shouts erupt throughout the room, each member trying to out shout one another. In a booming room Melcore demands silence. As the room quiets Melcore continues. "We must ensure the survival of our race. We aren't strong any longer. Our people will hold off the Turiec for a time, but in the end, they will overwhelm us. Starting tonight with you Daus, the Weldon people will travel to the eastern cities. Meroth is far beyond any ones power but mine. And I will most likely fail in the end. But, I will gladly sacrifice myself to see as many of our people make it away as possible." Looking around one last time at the gathered council, Melcore instructs them.

"This will be the last time the council will gather together. Divide our people up into sections defending the walls; if you hear the ice bells ringing, then you know the defenses have fallen. Each one of you is responsible for getting as many out as you can. Pick scouts from your section and have them start leading small groups to the eastern cities. Starting tonight, Daus, you begin with a small group; they are already gathered by the south gate. Take the mountain passes to Thurgel; take warning to the cities before you head south. We need to bleed this army as much as we can before they take the castle. In the distance the council hears horns blowing and the ground rumbles and bucks under their feet.

"Daus do not wait, get to the gate now!" Melcore shouts. "Everyone to the walls, the Turiec attack sooner than I thought!" Melcore bounds past the startled council members, striding down the stairs. Daus is right behind him, running for the gate. Coming out of the tower Melcore sees his people dazed and confused, looking around in shock. In a commanding voice, Melcore rallies his people into action.

"To the walls, to the walls, defend the city!" Spurring his people on Melcore seems to grow in power and stature the closer he gets to the battlements. Flying up the last stairs to the castle walls, everyone shrinks away from Melcore presence as he reaches the wall and looks down upon the ice fields. Spreading out on the plain as far as he can see are the Turiec people. As one they chant for the death of the Weldons. In the fore of the massive army is Meroth, resplendent in his jet black armor. Two figures of power look at each other. With a bellowing command, Meroth releases his army. With a great rush of bodies, the Turiec start the onslaught.

Bracing against the sudden attack, Melcore commands the bowmen to release devastation onto the enemy. In groups of eight, Weldon soldiers release their missiles. A fiery arc of arrows burst upon the Turiec. They hit their mark; each Turiec is enveloped in a blue fireball. Little does it slow the advancing army, there are ten more waiting to takes its spot. Looking out over the fields, Melcore starts to form a plan, thinking how much longer they have until they are overrun.

An hour passes by as the Weldons fight back the enemy. As quickly as it began, Meroth calls his people back. Below the castle wall lie hundreds of dead and dying Turiec. Melcore looks around seeing no Weldons hurt, he silently prays to his ancestors. Far out in the distance the people hear a great groaning sound. Coming down the plains is an unimaginable creature. At first it is hard to make it out, but as it draws closer, Melcore, stumbles back from the edge. Raising his hands to his face in disbelief, Melcore cries out in an ancient tongue, none but him can understand. Over the ice fields lumbers a giant of a figure. A grey creature close to a hundred feet tall strides towards the castle. Out of its upper body four huge arms sprout. Scales cover its chest, with a layer of black fur covering its lower body.

Swiftly turning around, Melcore sees a council member, rushing over to him, he commands her. "Go to the rest of the council members; tell them to double the evacuation to the cities!" Hurriedly, she runs down the battlement.

Looking out over the plains, Melcore knows it is just a matter of time before the castle walls are broken open. In the dying light, the enemy settles back, waiting for the coming day of retribution.Melcore stands vigil on the walls, in the dying light the Weldons see countless lights start to flare on the ice field. The day he has dreaded is coming to pass. He stands there hoping his people have time to flee across the mountains.

Standing on the battlements, Melcore waits for the next attack to be launched. Black clouds have rolled in from the north through the night, lightning dances in the distance steadily drawing closer. No sun will shine onto this barren land today thinks Melcore. Runners have reported to him that during the night, everyone except the defenders have gotten out of the city. It is up to them to bleed this army before they are defeated.

Down on the floor of the plain, Melcore can see movement as the massive army gathers together for the next assault. The Weldons nervously wait for the oncoming attack. Looking around at his people, Melcore silently prays they can hold out one more day to give his people a better head start through the mountain passes. As the castle waits, a low hum starts coming from the army below. Melcore sees a figure all too familiar walking through the mass of bodies. Silently waiting for Meroth, Melcore walks to the edge of the battlement looking down. On the field of battle, the dead Turiec have frozen in the night. Covering them in a thick layer of ice, making the field look as if hundreds of their enemies are looking up from under the ground at them, Meroth calmly walks toward the castle.Meroth approaches the walls calling up to the leader of the Weldon.

"Melcore, you and your people are hopelessly out numbered, come out and we will give you a quick death. Resist and face eternal suffering. Seeming to be standing on the edge of a precipice, Melcore looks down upon Meroth feeling as if he is a child in front of the gods being scolded. He feels power emanating from Meroth in waves. Melcore stands there being battered by a mystical wind assuredly as a hurricane was bearing down on him. Finally drawing the courage to confront this power, he draws himself up to his full height facing the monster.

"Meroth, you are the father of all evils visited upon on people. I will never barter with the like of you. Go back to the cold lonely hell of a world that suits you. We will fight you and your kind until the bitter end." In a fit of rage upon hearing this from his enemy Meroth strides forward on the ice field showering the barrier with bolts of lightning. Unable to penetrate it with his powers, Meroth turns to his army, commanding them to attack.

Thousands of Turiec pour forth towards the castle walls. For hours they break upon the walls like waves against a coast, The Weldons fire volleys of Ice bolts into them, sending many to the frozen ground. The Turiec slowly move closer toward the walls as the morning wears on. Looking out from the castle walls, Melcore studies the monster that has been summoned. Waiting for its' first approach. Only in legend has he heard of this beast. Once, late in the morning Melcore is summoned to a portion of the western wall. The Turiec have grabbed a foothold on the base of the castle, scaling the immense wall. Melcore looks down upon the Furious Turiec. They have climbed halfway up the outer wall. Melcore sends ice careening down onto the enemy. In seconds the Turiec are frozen in a layer of ice, never to move again.

Suddenly, shouts from the inner wall erupt. Melcore rushes to the battlement lining the outer wall looking down into the courtyard below. Squads of Turiec run by, striking down Weldons. A member of the council runs up to Melcore, "Lord, the Turiec have scaled the mountains to the east of us, they are pouring into the inner city." Feeling the last of his energy ebb, Melcore knows that the time has come. Slowly walking over to the outer battlement Melcore sees the monstrous figure advancing upon the city. Turning to the remaining people on the castle walls, Melcore commands them. "My people the outer wall has fallen, leave now, go to the eastern cities."

Telenor looks at his face, studying the lines, staringback into her eyes Melcore tells her. "Do what you can to get as many out as you can, but go to Melnin. See that our people have warning of our defeat." Looking at Melcore with love and respect Telenor says "Melcore you will be remembered for your sacrifice today!" With a small weary smile Melcore turns back to the enemy resigned to his fate.

Telenor makes her way down the stairs to the outer courtyard, compelling all Weldons to follow her. Soon Melcore is left standing alone on the battlement as the Turiec overwhelm the outer defenses. Melcore slowly rises into the air, moving over the outer wall ascending towards the ice fields. Looking out over his enemies, he sees the giant figure coming closer over the plain. On the ice field, the Turiec move back from the two figures, one towering over the other. Looking down upon Melcore, it slowly lumbers towards him. The ground shakes beneath him; he seems such a small figure on the plain. Turiec soldiers form a solid ring around them.

Melcore is standing in a sea of calm, surrounded by his enemy. He studies the abomination as it moves closer to him. From all around him, Melcore hears the Turiec people chanting. The creature seems to build strength from them, growing in size as it approaches him from across the ice field. Melcore slowly unsheathes his ruin carved longsword from his back. Looking upon the Malodor he focuses on making himself calm. Melcore closes his eyes, bringing images of ruins to his mind, quickly discarding them one at a time. Choosing a long set of ruins he opens his eyes making them appear in a floating circle around his head. Slowly they rotate around him faster and faster. They quicken there pace until a blur of ruins rotates around his head,

Melcore slowly grows with the passing seconds. Frothing in
rage the malodor bellows in an ancient tongue. It launches
itself towards Melcore, hitting an invisible wall. Melcore grows
tothirty feet tall; swinging his sword in an arc around his head,
he motions for a ruin to fly towards the beast. With a bellow
of pain a bolt of red fire hits the creature in the lower torso.
Instantly it bursts into flame. Black oily smoke erupts from the
creature has it stumbles back from the pain. Singed hair and
masses of bubbling skin falls from the creature in great globs,
dropping his barrier, Melcore launches himself against the beast,
his sword slashing a furrow across its thigh.

Recovering, the beast swings heavily down, taking Melcore
in the chest with a great punch of its lower arm. Melcore is
propelled backwards towards the Turiec army. Stumbling,
Melcore falls upon an invisible wall in front of him. He feels
himself smash into the barrier as current of yellow energy course
through him. In pain, Melcore throws himself off the barrier;
He feels hands close around his throat while he is lifted from
the ground. Unable to move Melcore feels life slowly draining
from him. The creature pushes Melcore against the barrier,
as great energies pulse through him. Melcore screams out in
pain. Still holding onto his sword, he twists in the grasp of the
creature. The point of his sword finds resistance as he shoves
it backwards behind him. With all his strength Melcore thrusts
blindly against the point.

He starts feeling the hands around his throat spasm and
slightly the pressure grows less. With a bellow of rage Melcore
twists his blade up. He is heavily dropped to the ground as the
creature releases its hold on him. Lying on the ground Melcore
transforms back into his normal size. He slowly painfully gets
back to his feet, looking around the battlefield. He sees the beast
a little distance off, blood is welling out of its chest in spurts.

Slowly, the chanting stops and the beast,s movements stop. Looking around he sees the figure of Meroth approaching him.

Feeling weakened by his struggle with the beast Melcore knows his death is upon him. Bringing his sword to bear, he prays to his ancestors. "Melcore, you did better than I thought you would against my child, but now your end is near." With a wave of his hand, Meroth envelopes Melcore in a solid blue light. Instantly Melcore freezes, he sees the world go dark. In his mind's eye he can see Meroth standing in front of him, with a slow smile spreading across his face. "Welcome to your new home Melcore. You didn't think I was going to outright end your life did you? I am going to put you on the castle wall as a lesson for those that confront me. To be dead, but not dead you shall spend the rest of eternity looking out over the north. Wondering how many of your people survive. Who knows, maybe from time to time I will visit you. Telling you about how your people died in agony."

Meroth comes to the front of his people gathered upon the plain.

"Oh my children, our home is open to us, enter the castle and kill all that remain!"

Chapter Nine
Britannia

Ranwulf stands in the window, wondering where to go. Looking back into the cottage he sees Nellian and Mariale staring at him. "Nellian, how long until Balian is able to travel" Ran asks of her.

Looking up at Ran, Nellian answers him. "Ranwulf, Balian will not be able to travel for weeks at the earliest." Walking back to the fire, Ran slumps at the table. With a sigh, Mariale comes over to Ran, putting her hand on his shoulder. "Ran, what can I do to help you?" Jerking away Ran stands up moving back to the window. "Mariale, you have already suffered enough on my count. I have to leave you two here. Balian needs to heal and I won't ask you to leave him. I've seen how you two look at each other. Mariale, stay here and take care of him." Looking towards Nellian, Ran wonders how she has lived here so long. "Nellian, where do you buy stuff you need?"

A little confused Nellian answers, "If I can't grow them here, I go into Wilot. It's a few miles inland, why?" With a thought, Ran answers. "Well, Nellian, I thought it might be a good idea and take a look around to see what's around here, after all we can't stay here forever." Nellian walks over to the window. "Just be careful Ranwulf, the Melcarens patrol the island. They most likely have no idea who you are, but be careful anyway."

Looking at MarialeRan smiles, "Mariale, stay here while I am gone and take care of him." With a sad smile on her face Mariale grabs Ran in a hug. Without looking at him, Mariale turns back to Balian with tears in her eyes. Nellian takes Ran by the hand leading him outside the small cottage. Ran starts walking round the corner of the dwelling, Ran looks to Nellian, taken back he sees she is once again a beautiful young lady.

Looking at him, Nellian leads him to the other side of her house. "Ran, remember when your around anyone you can't do anything out of the ordinary. No one here can do what you can. You will only draw the Melcarens to you."

Looking into the distance Ran replies, "Nellian, I just feel that I need to see what this land is like, what the people are like here. I feel lost, hopefully I can find—I don't know, and maybe I can find part of myself here." Looking at Ran with empathy Nellian turns and walks back to the cottage without saying a word.

After watching Nellian walk back to the cottage, Ran walks heading inland and hopefully to answers. Making his way across the plateau with the cold wind whipping at him, Ran wonders about his childhood. He has so many questions. Who is he, where did he really come from? All he has known of his life is the cold bitter land of Weldon. Looking across the countryside he walks, he notices a well-worn trail. Ran walks for most of the day, struggling against the strong winds coming from the coast. In the late afternoon he crosses a small hill. He sees he is on top of a hill looking down at a small town. A thick haze of grey smoke surrounds it. Even from here he can smell the foul stench. Surrounding it are tall rock walls with a wooden gate on the north side. Partway down each wall is a tower jutting out from the wall. He can see soldiers walking across the walls in twos' and threes'. He's never seen so many people gathered.

Ran, follows a trail down the hill coming up to the western side of the town. Small groups of people are camped out on the flat grass surrounding the town. Walking towards the gathered camps Ran sees a wide muddy road meandering among the tents and wagons haphazardly strewn around the walls. He can see people staring out of tents and wagons at him, shrinking back when he meets their gaze. Others are calling out to him, offering all sorts of goods. Ran walks away quickly on the side of the muddy road towards the gate. As he approaches the large wooden gate, a soldier wearing the Melcaren tabard calls to him. "You, come here." Stopping Ran looks up at him; he can see the soldier is not much older than him.

Sheepishly walking over to him, Ran keeps his head lowered staring at the ground. "Yes Sir?' The soldier spreads his feet and throws his shoulders back, he appraises him sharply. "What are you doing here? Tell the truth now, I can tell you don't have two pence's to rub together." Standing on one foot Ran answers. "Master, I was cold and hungry. I am looking for a place to sleep and food."

Looking towards the gate, the soldier motions Ran to the city. "Well you're in luck boy, stay here!" Walking a few paces the soldier waves toward the gate, in a few moments a squad of soldiers comes trotting towards them. The leader of the squad briskly walks up to Ran looking him over. "Good job Belliar, this young lad will do fine." The officer grabs Ran by the shoulder pushing him towards the squad. "Ok, you whelp, start moving, this is your lucky day! You just signed up for the Melcaren army." Ran, quickly looks up at the Melcaren officer. Catching the sudden reaction the officer cuffs Ran on the side of the head, sending him to the muddy ground. The squad laughs at him, sprawled in the road. Get up dirt bag; you're going to learn to listen to me. Hurriedly getting up Ran falls in beside the soldier, walking into the town, silently wondering at this what's going to happen and how he can possibly get away. Belliar takes a meandering path through the close streets through the town. Coming up to a small squat one room building, Belliar takes Ran by the arm propelling him through the door. Inside is a desk off to the side. Ran sees one soldier sitting at it with papers in front of him. The soldier looks up at Ran smiling a crookedly. "Belliar you have done well lately. I see you have another recruit for the cause." Pointing at Ran the soldier asks him, "Boy, What is your name and age?" Before Ran can answer Belliar cuffs Ran in the side of the head again. "Answer him now, Boy!"

"My name is Ran, sir. I am nineteen." Ran stands there, looking at the floor waiting for another cuff. "Alright, boy, go with Belliar and he will deliver you to your commander. Do well and you shall one day thank us for this chance to serve your nation." Belliar grabs Ran by the arm propelling him back out the building. The soldier pulls Ran along the dirty muddy streets until they reach a long low building on the southern side of the town. Going through the entranceRan sees rows of beds against the walls with a few soldiers at tables in the center of the room.

Belliar calls to one shoving Ran onto the floor. "Delk, take our new recruit and get him cleaned up and dressed properly." Jumping up from a table Delk hurries over to Ran. "Yes Belliar." Belliar turns around heading back to the door, then stops and glares at Ran. "Listen boy, don't try to escape or do anything stupid or you will be sorry!" with a look at Delk, Belliar leaves. Delk reaches down helping Ran up from the floor. Looking at him with sympathy Delk points at a door in the back of the building, "What's your name?" he asks Ran. Looking at DelkRan answers. "It's Ran sir." Motioning to the back Delk responds. "It's not sir, name is Delk. Go in the back and pick out a uniform like mine. Then take a bath and come back out." Looking closely into Rans' eyes he tells him. "Listen Ran; don't try to escape or anything. If you do we will be punished for it. Just do what you're told and things shouldn't be too hard on you." Nodding at Delk, Ran walks to the back room. Going through the door Ran sees piles of Melcaren uniforms on tables and round wooden bath tubs with steaming water in them. Looking through the uniforms he finds a set that fits him good. Quickly getting cleaned up and changed, he heads back out to the common area, wearing the white and red of the Melcaren army.

Ran sees Delk setting at a table eating. Delk motions for Ran to join him. Sitting down at the table, Ran is given a bowl of gruel and hard bread. "Eat Ran, we go on patrol this evening, you won't have a chance to eat until tomorrow." Ran delves into the gruel with a vengeance. He sees Delk looking at him after he finishes and looks back with a question on his face. "Listen Ran, I don't know where you are from. But, if you do something rash like trying to escape or not following orders, then we all pay, not just you. So, get any notions out of your head. We will stop you before that will happen, just do what you're told and when and things will be better off for you."

Looking around, Ran brings up the courage to ask Delk, "What are we doing here and what's going to happen to me?" Looking back at Ran, "Well, Ran you're in the Melcaren army whether you like it or not. Our job is to patrol our part of this land and do what we are told."

Before he can ask anything else Belliar comes through the door. "Form up men, it is time for patrol. The small squad of soldier jumps up, Delk takesRan by the arm leading him outside into the muddy street. The patrol is forms up in rows of two. Belliar looks at each of them, stopping when he comes to Ran, "Well then, I see you are listening boy, good. We will be heading inland; there are reports of disturbances some miles from here. Keep up and keep a look out." Without another word Belliar leads the squad through the narrow streets quickly heading through the northern gate. Within minutes they start a quick jog. Coming up over the hill to the west of the town, Ran looks back wondering how is to get away and wishing he had stayed back with his friends. The last thought he thinks before the pace quicken to a tortuous run is how are his friends going to find him?

For hours the small squad jogs away from the town into the hills of this cold land. Ran sees nothing but hills and rocks has far as the eye can see. They take a meandering course south into the mainland. Finally they stop, Delk looks over at Ran. "Ran, keep walking for a few minutes or you'll start to cramp up. Remembering his words earlier, Ran does what he is told, without any warning Belliar commands them to form up and the long tortuous run again. As they make progress south Ran notices that they have to zigzag back and forth as the land is broken by small fens and quagmires. Heading more to the west, Ran sees a small forest in the distance, getting a glance every so often over a low hill. The getting more hilly, travelling through the night, they make it to the edge of the forest about dawn. Belliar calls a stop. "Alright everyone, make what camp we can we will wait a few hours then head into the forest. I want to make it to Ferriost by tonight." Ran, slowly drops onto the ground with his back against a rock wall. Before he knows it, he is asleep.

A kick in the leg wakes him up. Belliar is standing over him. "Here boy, get up and eat while you have a chance." Looking around Ran sees the squad gathered around a small cook fire. Belliar motions Ran over. Ran goes over to the fire. A soldier gives him a small bowl of soup and some bread. Ran sees Delk a few yards off. Sitting on the ground next to Delk, Ran quietly eats, looking around every few minutes. Delk prods Ran on the shoulder, motioning him to finish. "It's time to go, break camp, Belliar commands them. In a flurry of activity they gather everything. In a few minutes they are formed back up heading towards the dark forest.

Coming up to the edge of the forest Ran sees they have come to a small road leading under it. Stopping the squad, Belliar walks up to Ran, He shoves a small wide sword in a scabbard at Ran. "Boy, belt this on, pray we don't need it in here." Ran belts the small sword around his waist. Walking to the front of the squad, Belliar tells them, "If we run into any renegades or other things keep close together and follow my commands! Does everyone understand?" Feeling eyes upon him, Ran looks up at him and nods. "Good, I want to make good time; we aren't stopping until we get to Ferriost." Ran looks around at the deep canopy over there head as they enter the forest. As they travel along the unbroken track through the forest Ran can hear branches break on each side every so often. He sees that Belliar has his broadsword drawn, his eyes going from one side of the forest to the other, constantly surveying where they are. Rans' body is starting to protest at the pace Belliar is forcing on them, and he can see a couple others starting to break stride. Suddenly Belliar goes down on the small road with a yell. The squad spreads out on either side of the road. Delk pulls Ran to his side. Ran looks towards Belliar wondering what's happening, understanding dawns on him as he sees an arrow sprouting from his shield.

From the forest, Ran can hear a voice calling to them. "Little soldier boys, where shall you go?"

Looking around Belliar calls back, "Forest dweller, go back to your cave and let us be!" Maniacal laughter can be heard coming from the forest. "Oh little Melcaren soldiers, you should have stayed home. The wintry wolves are coming for you!"

Jumping up Belliar shouts to his them, get up everyone, and follow me. Delk pulls Ran to his feet; quickly they are running down the road in a desperate attempt to flee. In the distance Ran can hear the insane laughter following them, taunting them. He feels his stomach go cold. From out of the forest some distance Ran hears the haunting call of wolves on the prowl. The hairs on the back of his neck stand up. Looking to the left through the brush Ran sees a fleeting silvery grey shape darting through the trees. "Beware the left" Belliar calls out. Seeing a large grey shape flying out of the forest, it takes the man in front of him, blood spraying everywhere as his throat is ripped open. As quickly as it is there the shape disappears into the underbrush. Ran feels a slap on his shoulder. "Ran, Move bellows Delk, Keep up or it's our death!" Seeing the squad moving away Ran doubles his run and they quickly catch up.

Coming around a bend in the road, they see a small cave on the other side of the road. "Quickly in there!" Belliar shouts. As they reach the edge of the cave Belliar feels himself go down under a pile of bodies. He hears the scream of a soldier as blood soaks him. Ran hears a muffled growl as he looks into the eyes of a monster. Standing over him is a Silvery grey wolf, easily standing five feet at the shoulders. The soldiers scramble away from him heading into the cave, leaving him alone. Looking down at him, Ran sees eyes the color of fire staring into his face. He feels drool falling down onto his face as the creature slowly brings its' muzzle close. Frozen in place unable to move under its baleful stare. The wolf bears its teeth as Ran feels a deep guttural growl erupt from its chest. Looking up, waiting for death Ran silently prays hoping it will end quickly.

Looking down at Ran on the ground the wolf slowly brings its muzzle to his face sniffing him. Suddenly with a growl of rage, the wolf raises its head calling in a long haunting howl. With one last look at Ran the wolf bounds away into the forest faster than an arrow, leaving Ran lying on the ground. The squads of soldiers silently stare at Ran. Ran quickly gets off the ground, half running, half crawling into the small cave, not sure why he was spared. The soldiers scurry away from Ran as he makes it into the cave. Belliar stares at Ran. Howls erupt from the forest all around them. Walking farther back into the cave, Belliar commands them to form a ring across the entrance of the cave. They spread out with swords drawn, waiting silently for the next attack. In the back of the cave Belliar lights a torch. "Pray to whatever gods you hold dear men."

Throughout the day, they are surrounded, unable to leave the cave. Without warning the howls of the wolves stop and silence ensues. The daylight is fading from the forest as night approaches. "Well men, it looks like we will be staying the night. Two of us left will take guard the entrance at a time. Delk you and Ran will take first watch. Yell, if you see anything." Ran follows Delk to the front of the cave, looking out at the dark forest. Ran can see the fallen soldier lying out in front of the cave. Delk and Ran exchange looks. They sit down on either side of the opening beginning there long vigil.

Looking into the forest Ran can hear movement, but can't see anything. Thinking back Ran starts to ponder why the wolf spared him. Delk comes over and prods Ran on the shoulder, looking up Delk points to the left of the cave. Looking out Ran doesn't see anything. Starting to look back at Delk, Ran sees in the corner of his eye a brief glimmer of yellow light. Quickly looking back, Ran can now see a flickering light bobbing up and down in the forest. Turning around Delk calls back into the cave, "Belliar, a light approaches from the forest road!" Quickly coming to the entranceBelliar looks out. "What new devilry is this?" he mutters. "Men weapons out, be ready!"

Forming in the front of the cave, they silently wait for the approaching light. After a few minutes they can see a number of flickering lights approaching in the distance. They can just make out clanking of metal on metal and the gruff voices of soldiers. Standing up in the entrance, Belliar calls out to them. With a relaxed pose, Belliar sheaths his sword and slowly walks from the cave. Coming around the last bend in the road a column of fifty Melcaren soldiers comes into view. They march up to the cave, the leader walks up to Belliar. Belliar salutes him sharply. "Soldier, what are you doing, hiding in a cave?" looking back at his squad he commands them to fall into.

"Sir, we were attacked on the road by the denizens of the forest; two of my men were killed by wolves. We simply sought refuge from them." Centurion Belliar responds. Looking around at the squad the centurion points to his column, "Well, soldier, follow along with us, we go to Ferriost, how many men do you have left?"

A soldier from his column approaches the centurion. "Centurion Antonius we must get moving, time is short." Standing there Ran tries to shrinks down hearing the commanders' name, looking back at the soldier he nods. Antonius looks at the small squad, his eyes coming to rest on Ran. With a quizzical look he begins to say something then shakes his head. Looking back at BelliarAntonius motions back to his soldiers. "Soldier, form up with us and stay close, there is a lot of activity in here tonight."

Saluting Antonius, Belliar moves his squad into the Ranks of the column. With a sharp command from the front, they are marching along the forest road. Looking around Ran sees Delk, Delk looks back and with a quick motion stalls any questions Ran may have. From the corner of his eye, Ran sees Antonius slowly walk back to his position in the column. Antonius walks alongside Ran, studying him. Looking at Ran he commands him, "Soldier, come here." Stepping out of the column Ran follows alongside Antonius with Belliar looking at them. "What is your name soldier?" Antonius asks him. Belliar scrambles over to Antonius answering for him. "His name is Ran, Sir; we picked him up in Perot." Quickly looking at Belliar, Antonius strikes him knocking him to the grounds. "I did not ask you soldier, mind your place and get back in line." Belliar rushes back into the formation glaring at Ran. "Where do you come from young man?" Antonius questions him.

Trying to think quickly Ran's memories of his mother comes to him. "I ran away from my mother and father's farm north of here, sir." Ran answers him. Looking at Ran with a look Antonius gives him an appraising look, "So, you didn't like living at home, eh? Come south to join the army boy." Staring forward Ran answers, "Yes, sir."

Antonius looks back at Ran with a question then thinks better of it, "Get back in the column soldier, Welcome to the army." Without another glance Antonius strides to the front of the column. Ran hurries back into place next to Delk. Through the remainder of the night the soldiers march along the forest road, chanting in caddice, quickly eating up the miles through the forest. Every so often Ran looks back, seeing Belliar glaring at him.

By the morning the column leaves the forest, the land transforming into farmland. On either side of the road, they pass farmers in wagons taking their stock to town. Ran, glances around as they pass the wagons, trying to think if he could possibly slip away and hide in one of them. Looking to the left he sees Antonius staring at him, dashing all hopes of escape. Antonius motions to him, and a soldier walks up to Ran. "Soldier, follow me."

Ran follows the Melcaren back to Antonius. Walking alongside his men, Antonius looks at Ran. "Walk beside me soldier. You see these fields along the road?" Ran looks to Antonius puzzled. "I was raised in a farm like these we pass. Now after many years I command an army of men. Do you know why? Well I will tell you." Antonius points to Rans' forehead. "There soldier, because I used my head, I Ran away from home at an early age like you too. I see myself in you, when I was your age. I am going to take you under my guidance and give you a chance at a great life soldier." Turning towards his captain Antonius motions him over. "Captain, This soldier will be reassigned to me immediately."

Looking at Ran, Antonius tells him, "Walk with me Ran and listen." As the column travels through the countryside approaching Ferriost Antonius tells Ran of his life in the army, slowly explaining to Ran what he needs to do in the army.

Walking along with the enemy, Ran wonders how his life could have changed so fast and so much in such a short amount of time. "You see Ran; I was lost when I was your age. I wanted to belong to something greater than myself. In our country nothing is more important than service. You were raised in a barbaric land, not knowing what it means to belong to a great cause. I will teach you the meaning of belonging to something great. I am a commander of many men and will teach you to take my part. We protect the borders of our country from terrible enemies. In the south we have the southern kingdom encroaching upon our lands, while in the west; the beasts of the wild continually pillage our land. When I look to the north I see a great despicable people, always looking to the south. Evil flows from them in great gouts. In ancient times we banished them to the cold north, but we can't rest until they are destroyed forever. One day they will come back to this land, when that happens we must be ready." Looking around at the soldiers in under his command, Ran sees just dejected people being forced into a way of life.

As Antonius keeps talking, Ran looks up at him. Thinking of all the stories he was told growing up. Looking around at the soldiers, he realizes that they don't hate him or the Weldons for any certain reason; it is the men that rule them that are afraid. Listening to Antonius he knows what he must do; He will follow Antonius and become a Melcaren soldier. He needs to know more about them. Ran realizes that his people will not survive in the southern lands without its people understanding who they are. That will not happen until the rulers of this land change. Memories from the past surface, he has seen the same way of thinking from the high council of his people, for reasons unsaid, he is being chased. Walking straighter beside Antonius; Promising silently to himself that he will change the way the Weldons and Melcarens' look at each other.

The city walls of Ferriost come into view. Great stone walls rise up from the plain. Unlike the last city, no people are camped out in front of the walls. He faces shining white walls, made out of granite. Clean kept grass runs straight to the high stone walls. The column marches to the city gates, in Rans' astonishment the gates are made from metal, brilliantly polished. Silently swinging open upon their approach, the Melcaren troop passes beneath them. Looking back Ran sees his last chance of escape receding as the gates slam shut behind him.

Antonius leads his soldier to the docks by the bay. Ships are already for them. The column stops near the first dock; Antonius breaks away, giving commands to his captains. Taking Ran in tow, they make their way onto a large battle galley at the front of the assembled ships. Ran is led onto the ship, being told to do as he was commanded by the captain. Antonius makes his way into a cabin in the front of the ship. Quickly, Ran is helping the sailors to raise the main sails. Within a short period of time, the small fleet is moving out into the bay making its way to the mainland. Quietly Ran stands there looking back to shore, panicking. How will he ever find Mariale and Balian again? A shift in the wind pulls the ships forward, causing Ran to fall as the sailor laugh. The ships' captain approaches Ran with a toothy grin. Quickly raising to his feet, Ran at him.

Ran is stunned as the captain knocks him to the ground. "You've been given into my care boy, that's your first lesson of the day. When I approach you, you had best be busy working." Stumbling to his feet, Ran makes his way to the sails to help the others tie them off. The captains' head snaps around as he points to another sailor. "Hey, you little land rat, you're doing that wrong. Come here." His voice trails off as Ran looks forward seeing Antonius standing in the window of his cabin staring at him. Quickly turning away, Ran wonders how he is going to survive.

Chapter Ten
The Chase

Derhuick wakes hearing Feal arguing with the scouts. Hurrying into the main room Derhuick sees Feal being restrained by two of them. "What is going on out here?" Derhuick asks. Feal stops resisting. "Derhuick get these two off me now!" Derhuick motions to them. Feal looks at Derhuick with a glare," I am going back to the north, do you hear me Derhuick." Looking around at his scouts he sees one of them pointing into a room. "Sis, a man came to us a few minutes ago from the castle." Looking at Feal Derhuick tells her. "Feal, just calm down and wait a minute. Let me talk to him." without looking back Derhuick walks into the room, seeing a figure lying on a bed, with blood welling from a cut in his side. He sees Feal walk into the room coming to his side. "Daus tell Derhuick what you told me." Looking at Derhuick a low moan escapes from Daus' mouth. Derhuick can see a small trickle of blood from his lips; He knows he is just moments from death. Derhuick walks up to the bed kneeling next to Daus. Looking at him, Derhuick waits for him to speak.

"Derhuick, the city has fallen." Daus tells him. "Our people have fled east through the mountain passes." Stunned Derhuick grabs his hand. "Daus, What do you mean? Our city has fallen, who attacked us and why?"

Looking away from him, Daus starts coughing heavily. As he looks back to him Derhuick sees the anguish in his eyes. "Derhuick, the Turiec attacked us. I was told to come find you by Melcore. He said...he said to tell you and Feal that by the time I had found you...that the city would be gone and our people would be fleeing east."

Derhuick looks away, turning to Feal he looks at her eyes. He sees tears streaming down her cheeks. "Derhuick, we must go back and try to help them!" Feal says. Looking back at Daus, Derhuick questions him. "Daus, What else were you told?" Derhuick, Melcore told me…to tell you and Feal that you must find Ranwulf…" Sharply looking at FealDerhuick motions her outside. Feal feeling like she had been dismissed as an errant child, stomps away to the inner room.

"Daus, Where is Melcore?" Derhuick asks him. "Derhuick, Melcore went stayed…to face Meroth…he sent me with a small group…out, I am the only one left alive…everyone else that… went with me is dead…"

Looking at Daus, Derhuick feels the agony in his voice. Daus begins to cough heavily, blood welling up in a bigger stream flecked with bubbles. His body spasms and he sits up. "Derh…Melcore said you must find the boy…he said…he's our only hope." With a great spasm, Daus falls back to bed, his life flowing away from his body. Bowing his head Derhuick prays a silent prayer for Daus and their people. Slowly standing, Derhuick makes his way back to the inner room. Coming up to the fire, Derhuick grabs a pot, throwing it across the room in a great crash against the far wall. A soldier jumps up, being scolded from the water.

Looking over at Feal, Derhuick slowly approaches her, "Feal, no matter what you want to do, we have to find this boy, Now more than ever." In horror Feal looks at Derhuick. "What are you talking about; we need to go help our people." Standing up, Derhuick addresses his scouts. "Everyone, get ready to leave in a few minutes, we continue the hunt for this boy. Feal, whether you agree or not with the course, you have your order from Melcore." Staying at him Feal acknowledges her duty. "I know that Derhuick! When I find this boy, he will pay dearly for this chase!"

Quickly gathering their supplies together the scouts leave the tree, heading south towards the plains. Moving among the forest they search for signs of their prey. Looking around at the under growth Feal notices that the pants seem to be moving behind them as they pass. "Derhuick, look behind us, do you see our trail?" Without looking Derhuick tells her. "No Feal, that's a thing about this forest, as you travel through it, your path disappears."

Looking to the south Feal, stops and closes her eyes. Feeling the presence of the three, east of them, Feal turns to Derhuick. "Derhuick, they have headed east why are we going south?" Looking back her, Derhuick responds "Feal, we need to make good time, which means we need to get to the open planes and travel them, as much as possible. Now, please stop talking." They travel in silence for the rest of the day as the miles slog by. Near evening, they come upon the southern edge of the forest. Derhuick motions for the scouts to wait. Derhuick silently walks up to the edge looking out over the plains. He hears a branch break behind him, spinning around, he pins Feal to the ground with a dagger at her throat. Instantly seeing it is Feal, Derhuick growls and motions for her to get down. Over the low hills they hear the pounding of hooves as a large column of soldiers gallop past. After a few moments Derhuick takes Feal deeper into the trees. "Feal, you are not in the north anymore, if you want to see the sun come up tomorrow, then do what I say. The lands here are not like Weldon. Everybody here is the enemy!" With a disgusted look Derhuick walks off, into the trees towards the other scouts. Silently curses at him, Feal starts to follow him when she hears a grunt up ahead and shouting coming from the scouts.

Feal sees Derhuick running back towards her, "Feal, run!" Without a backward glance Feal runs south into the open plains as Derhuick and the other scouts catch up. Derhuick motions to a small rocky hill a couple hundred yards from them. In a spurt of movement they make it to the small hill, diving behind it. Crawling to the side of it they see a small group of men crouched in the edge of the forest unwilling to follow them into the plain. Most of them have bows drawn, in a few minutes they creep back into the forest.

"Well, Derhuick, what now, we are in the plains and can't travel the forest," Feal asks. Looking around at the dying light, Derhuick motions to one of his scouts, "Go east and scout the area out, if you see anything come back and tell us. We will follow after you in a few moments." The scout quickly moves of into the distance, a small low figure moving in a d out of view among the low hills. Derhuick signs to the remaining scouts motioning for them to spread out and head east. Looking over at Feal he motions her to follow him. "Feal, we just lost two of our scouts in there; we will have to follow the forest from the edge as long as we can." Throughout the night, they make their way along the outskirts of the forest. Shortly before dawn, they hear the galloping of hooves has the lead scout returns to the group. He motions to Derhuick the direction of the approaching party. Derhuick tells Feal to get back to the forest as they regroup. Quickly, they move into the edge of the forest as the horses gallop past them from a distance. Looking around Derhuick can see mountain tops in the far distance.

"Feal, we have many days of travel and need to stay in the shadow of the forest, the Melcaren people heavily patrol this part of the forest. If those three are heading east, they will run into a large ocean. Either we will catch them there or if by some chance they get across, the island across is small, making it easier to find them."

They travel for the next few days by night, soon, Feal can smell an odd smell and the breeze gets colder. Seeing her strange look Derhuick points to the east, "We are within a few days of the coast, that is what you smell Feal. We have to be really careful now. In a day or two we are going to be near a town by the coast." Without looking back Derhuick hurries the scouts farther east, setting a hard pace for Feal to keep up with.

Before dawn that night, Derhuick stops the scouts at the edge of the forest. He motions to them to gather as the sun makes its' way up over the tree tops. "Alright, we are within a few hours of Foult. Feal and I are going into town. The rest of you need to make camp and wait for us to return." Turning to Feal, Derhuick asks her. "Feal, can you tell which way the boy is?" Concentrating Feal looks spins around. "He is east and north of us Derhuick, Why?" Looking exasperated Derhuick answers, "Because Feal, that means they are across the sea and on the island." Nodding Feal walks into the edge of the forest, sitting down she tries to relax her aching muscles.

Waking up with a touch on her shoulder, she sees Derhuick standing over her. "Feal, it's time to go." Gathering herself together, Feal follows Derhuick out into the plain leaving the rest of the scout behind. After a few minutes, they come upon a road cut through the plain. Straight and level it runs across the plain. Turning onto it, they travel eastward. "Feal, I know we have our problems, I know you don't like me in the least, but if you want to complete this mission you will have to listen to me. I know this land and you Do Not." He says as he stops and looks at her.

"Derhuick, I realize that, I just don't trust you. I don't trust your motives. You seem to be more of a southern now than a

Weldon." Derhuick points back to the north. "Feal, after the battle, we all are or will soon be Southern. That's why I was sent here years ago. To spy out this land against the day we had to return. Now, Feal, when we get into town, do not talk unless I say it is ok. It is the custom for a husband to speak for his wife." Red color floods her cheeks as she stares at him.

Feal bites her lip as she glares at him. "Fine, Derhuick, I will do as you request, let's just get this over with." Feal strides down the road with Derhuick silently laughing as he follows her. For the next couple of hours they see no one, then as the come closer to the outskirts of the town, the salty smell grows strong and they start seeing farms on either side of the road. A few people stare at them as they pass on the road, but hurry past without a word. The day would have been hot without the gusty wind from the coast. Clouds are rolling in from as they come over the top of a hill and see a large city sprawled out in front of them. It is easily two miles wide and as deep. In the distance, Feal can see ships of great size floating in from the harbor towards the city. On the field in front of it, masses of people are gathered in disarray. More tents than she can count are set up before the city walls. Up and down the road leading into the city are columns of soldiers on horseback. The people give them room as they pass, with some calling out to them as they pass.

Silently, Feal and Derhuick walk down the road into the outskirts. Many unknown smells and sights confront Feal as they make their way through crowds of people milling around. Derhuick keeps hold of her hand as they wind their way towards the city gate. Coming up to it, Derhuick sees it is closed against the crowd. Looking up at the gate, Derhuick impatiently calls out, Woe the gate seek to gain entrance into the city. Looking at the immense gate, Derhuick sees a small window open from within. A small chubby face framed in brown hair sticks his head out. Quickly looking around, the fellow says. "Leave this area before I have you arrested." Before he can shut the window Derhuick calls out. "Helui, open the door and let me in!" Looking down Helui squints down into the crowd. "Derhuick is that you? What are you doing coming in from this entrance?" Looking at Helui Derhuick answers. "Open the door and I will tell you."

A small door open at the base of the gate, moving the crowd back, Derhuick and Feal squeeze in. In the dim light of a small tunnel Feal sees a middle aged man, chubby with a perpetual smile on his face. Clasping Derhuick in a bear hug, Helui looks over at Derhuick motioning towards Feal. "She is my newest Eosin Helui." Nodding at him he motions them inside the room in the gate. Sitting down at a table Helui pulls out a feather, writing their names on it. "Where are you headed Derhuick, its' been long since you traded around here?" With a smile Derhuick looks bemused. "Helui, how long have we been friends? Ten years or more, why the questions." Taken back by memories Helui looks at Derhuick, "I'm sorry old friends, there trouble up north. Some sort of mischief with the forest dwellers and northerners." Relaxing, Derhuick points to Feal, "Well, her father has commissioned me to go to Britannia and trade for some rare wines."

A noise at the door brings the conversation to a stop as a soldier walks in. "Helui, stop jabbering and get to the gate, we will be opening them soon." Getting up, Helui shakes his friend's hand. "Well, when you get a chance come over for dinner later this week, I trust you remember where I live, old friend." Standing up Derhuick moves toward the door. "Of course, we will Helui." Quickly they move out the door and head into town. "So, that's how you move around so easily here, you're a trader." Smiling at Feal Derhuick only looks back and walks along the city streets. They make their way through the crowded street; soon lights flicker on, that are mounted on poles lining the street. Near dark, they follow the street onto the dock. Walking along it for some distance, Derhuick follows a small dock out over the water coming up to the graceful bow of a small ship. He is greeted by a Melcaren on board. "Master, welcome back, we did not expect you." Walking up the plank to the ship, Derhuick shakes hands with him. "Thank you, Astor. Please get the crew together; I need to head to Britannia by the morning." With a quick salute, Astor walks down to the dock heading off into the night.

Looking around at the graceful ship, Feal sees Derhuick in a new light. "You seem to have done well for yourself here, who are you exactly Derhuick in this strange land?" Slowly looking around at his ship, Derhuick responds. "I am a simple trader of good and services Feal, nothing more. Why position gives me the freedom to travel this land." Looking sideways at him Feal smiles and says nothing. "Feal, go through that door and you'll find a room you can use." He says pointing towards the small cabin on the foredeck. Without a backwards glance Derhuick climbs the ladder to the main deck disappearing inside. Feal makes her to the foredeck. Quickly she disappears into the cabin. Entering the cabin she looks around is slightly surprised to see an opulent furnish suite given over to her. A large bed is on the side of the room with a finely carved writing desk littered with papers and notes. A golden wash basin and pitcher sits near the front window. Walking around the room she spies a closet, opening it, it is filled with ladies clothes all richly embroidered with silver and gold thread. Closing the closet doors, she walks over to the bed, planning just to sit down and rest. It is so soft she lies down for a second, enveloped in the feel of its comfort. Before, she knows it she is asleep.

Up in the wheel house, Derhuick pours over maps and writings for a time. Soon, he hears boots coming up on deck. Astor walks into the wheel house waiting for his master to speak. Looking up with a smile, Derhuick asks. "Is everyone accounted for Astor?' Smiling Astor replies. "Yes sir, we are waiting your command." Motioning for Astor to come over to him, Derhuick points to a place on the map. "Cast of as soon as you can, and make for this cove. I want to be there as soon as possible." Saluting him, Astor walks out on deck, yelling orders to the sailors. Soon the ship rocks with the waves as they pass silently out of the harbor.

Feal wakes to the gently rocking motion of the ship the following morning. She can hear sailors on deck, shouting back and forth as they sail across the water. Rising from the bed, she opens the door looking out across the deck. In the wheelhouse she can see Derhuick, talking with the man Astor. Seeing the door open, Derhuick points to Feal motioning her to go back inside her cabin, she quickly slams the door. Walking to the front of the cabin, she draws the curtain back, looking out she sees a grey cold ocean. In the distance she can see a small smudge of land. Behind her, the door opens and Derhuick quickly comes into the cabin. "So you have woken up Feal. Please stay in the cabin. I will have men bring you a bath soon and some food. Pointing to the closet, he tells her. "You will find better clothes in the closet. Please pick a suitable outfit and I will be back soon to join you for breakfast. As Feal is about to start talking, Derhuick puts his finger in front of his lips, "Remember what I said Feal, please don't talk. Even here we have to be careful, the walls have ears." With a smile on his lips Derhuick turns and leaves the cabin. He orders a bath and food for Feal. He walks back to his cabin on the main deck quickly bathing and changing in to a richly woven merchants outfit.

After a reasonable amount of time, Derhuick walks back to her cabin. Opening the door without announcing himself, he sees Feal setting down at the table eating breakfast. She had changed into a thickly woven dress with rich designs embroidered into it. Sitting down across the table from her, he smiles at her, for even though she is far different from him, she is still a beautiful lady. While he sits there eating breakfast, he can feel her eyes staring at him. Looking up he smiles, "I trust you slept well Feal?" Staring back she responds, "I slept well, now Derhuick, tell me where were going." Standing up, Derhuick walks over to the window, "Come here Feal," he says. As she walks over he points out through the window straight ahead of the ship. "That is Britannia, Feal. I mean to land on the eastern side of the island and head our prey off." Walking back to the table, Feal sits down to finish breakfast. After a moment, Derhuick walks up to her looking down her says, "Feal, please just stay in the cabin until we reach the island. We should be there in a few hours." With a nod, Derhuick walks out of the cabin, silently closing the door behind him. A moment later, Derhuick can hear something hard hit the door. Humming to himself, he walks back to the wheelhouse.

As evening approaches, a knock on the door brings Feal away from thoughts of her homeland. A moment later, Astor comes into the cabin. "Madam, Master Derhuick requests your presence on deck." Silently standing there, he makes it obvious it is a question. Standing up she follows Astor out onto deck, looking about she sees the crew hurriedly changing sails. Coming around the front of the cabin she sees Derhuick standing against the rail looking at the approaching land. She follows his gaze, as she walks up to his side she can see a shallow bay lined with tall trees. The ship is headed straight into it. Smiling at her, Derhuick points toward the far end of a bay where a dock is nestled against the shore. A rough plank walkway leads from the dock to a house set against the side of a small hill. Feal can see light lit in the house and smoke billowing from the fireplaces dotting the home. As they enter the bay the constant wind slacks and then stops as the ship bumps against the pier. Sailors quickly tie up to the pier, lowering the gangplank. With a nod to Feal, Derhuick takes her hand leading her quickly off the ship and up the walkway to the front door of the house. Looking around Feal sees a grandly made home looking out over the ocean. A full deck surrounds the home, while she can see bright light from inside and the sounds of activity come from within. Astor comes up the walkway opening the door beckoning for her to come in. Derhuick leads Feal into the front room. Sitting down by the fireplace he motions for Feal to join him. Looking at Feal Derhuick tells her "Feal, you should get plenty of sleep tonight; we will start into the city of Ferriost in the morning. There, I will see if I can find any trace of our prey. "Can you sense anything from them Feal?"

Concentrating, Feal tries to locate the boy, with a confused look on her face she turns to Derhuick, "What's wrong Derhuick, I can't see them?" Looking into the fire Derhuick contemplates it. "I'm not sure, it may be this land or maybe the boy is under someone protection, which just means that we will have to find him through normal means." Standing up Derhuick tells her. "I am going to sleep Feal; when you are ready, Astor will show you to your room."

The morning light brings Feal awake. She can hear the patter of rain drops on the window. Quickly getting up, she dresses in her plain pants and a thick tunic. Walking downstairs she sees the servants preparing for breakfast, one of them leads her into the front room. A fire is crackling and popping in the fireplace, she sits down on a chair next to Derhuick. Looking up at her Derhuick smiles, "I hope you slept well Feal, we have a long day ahead of us, and we need to get to Ferriost. I have contacts there, hopefully that will help finding them."

After a quick breakfast, they start towards Ferriost. During the morning the rain grows steadily heavier. Walking along the muddy tracks of the small road, they slither and slip up and down hills through the day. Looking south they can see a large storm brewing, thunder booms in the distance.

Chapter Eleven
Balian's Long Road

Balian slowly rises from his bed. A fire crackles in the middle of the room. Mariale and Nellian sit at the table alongside it. Tenderly walking over to the table Balian sits down next to Mariale. "Are you feeling better today Balian?" Nellian asks him. Sitting up straighter, Balian responds, "Yeah, I am feeling almost whole again." Stretching again, he can move without too much pain. Coming over to him, Nellian lifts his shirt, still seeing an angry black bruise slowly turning yellow greets her eyes.

Looking into his eyes Nellian admonishes him to be careful. Staring into the fire, Balian asks the question that is on both his and Mariale's mind. "Nellian, how long until you think it is ok for me to travel. We need to go after Ran!"

Looking at them both, Nellian replies. "Balian, I know you're worried, if you take it easy, you should be ok to leave. But, if you don't take it slow you will hurt yourself.I can't follow you inland. The only thing I can do is mask your trail from those that hunt you. I will give you clothes so you can fit in better here, but it is up to you two to find him. I can't take any direct role in this."

With a look at Balian asks him. "Are you sure you are able to travel, I don't want you do hurt yourself more." Looking at her Balian smiles, "I am ready if you are? Our friend needs us." Nellian walks over to them with two bags of food and small odds and ends. She gives these and clothes to them, quickly changing they say goodbye to the little girl in the cottage. As they walk through the door, her eyes glimmer with tears to see them go. Standing out in front of the cottage, they turn inland slowly making their way along the grassy plain. They walk through the day heading south. Away in the distance they can see a storm brewing, lightning bolts cross the sky in jagged arcs. In the distance they can see a forest surrounded in mist. "Balian, do you think we can make it to the forest by nightfall?" Mariale asks. Looking up at the dying light, Balian responds, "I don't know but, let's give it a try."

Picking up their pace, the slight drizzle turns into a steady downpour, making the way slick. More slipping and slithering meets them as they slowly make it across the hills. Sometime after dark, they make it to the edge of the trees. Walking along the forest edge, they find a trail going in after a few minutes. Mariale looks at Balian in apprehension, "I don't like the look of that, but I don't like the idea of spending the night under the rain either." With one last look back, they enter the trees cautiously. Walking a few yards into the underbrush, they move off the path and huddle together under the dry canopy. Looking at Mariale, Balian tells her, "Get some sleep, when I can't keep my eyes open I'll wake you." Snuggling against him, Mariale is soon asleep, feeling his heart beat in his chest.

In the dark of the night Balian can hear movement all around them. It is too dark to see more than a couple feet, but off away from them he hears branches breaking and low growls throughout the long night. Once, when a branch broke what seemed just feet away, he started to wake Mariale, but then heard something scurry off, not returning.

Finally after what seemed like eternity, Balian could make out the cold grey light of dawn coming through the treetops. Touching Mariales shoulder he quietly wakes her. "Mariale, it is time to go, dawn is coming." Coming awake, Mariale leans forward, slowly stretching. "Balian, you said you were going to wake me." She says. Looking at him, she sees the worry in his eyes, looking around she silently questions him. "It's alright,

I couldn't sleep, we should try to make some distance through this forest today, and I don't want to spend another night here." Quickly they move back to the trail following it deeper into the forest. The forest is different the one they travelled on the mainland. This one is wet and soggy, with moss hanging from the branches. Even in the day it is cold. Every so often in the distance they can hear branches breaking and muffled cries. Staying close to each other, they slowly make it across the forest floor, hoping to beat the sun to the other side.

After a few hours of walking, they come upon a larger path. Looking each way, they don't see anyone on it. Balian makes his way along the path for a few feet. Turning to Mariale he asks her, "Well, what do you think, we can definitely make better time on this." Looking back the way they came, she agrees with a nod. Without a word they hurry down the path. They can see a well-worn trail on the path from many feet.

Behind them they hear a branch breaking, swiftly turning; Balian sees a silvery shape disappear into the trees. Gripping Mariales hand he quickens their pace. Walking for a few minutes, they hear movement on the right side of the path. Turning Mariale sees a silvery shape following them off the side of the path. "Balian, did you see that?" Mariale asks him. Looking to the right and left, he responds. "Yes, Mariale, they have been following us for a while, let's just get out of here." Hurrying down the path, they come to a fork in it. To the right it opens to a regular road, travelling straight east through the forest. Looking at the fork, Balian points to the more open road, quickly pulling her after him. Walking along the road, they make better time, but, looking at Mariale, Balian knows they aren't going to make it out of the forest by nightfall.

"Mariale, I think we need to find a place for the night. It's getting late." Balian tells her. As they come over the top of a rise in the road, they stop still in the road. Facing them over the hill is a silver grey wolf easily standing five feet at the shoulders. Red baneful glowing eyes stare at them, Balian moves closer to Mariale, quickly pushing her behind him. He stares back at the creature, not sure what to do, He slowly pulls his dagger from his belt, knowing it'll be little help against a creature like this.

Before he can do anything, a deep growl comes from its chest before it slowly walks off into the forest, its glowing red eyes staring back at them. As if coming awake from a dream, Balian pulls Mariale after him hurrying down the road. "We really need to find a place to hide for the night."

Almost breaking into a run, they make it a couple miles before they slow down. Coming around a curve in the road they see off the side of the road a small cave. "Mariale, in there," They walk over to the entrance of the cave trying to see how far back it goes. In the entrance they see a sword lying on the floor of the cave. "Well, someone else had the same idea we do," Balian comments. In the distance they hear branches breaking. Looking out into the forest, they see three silver wolves come trotting into the road. Each of the stand atleast four feet at the shoulders, Mariale and Balian hear them growling as they approach the cave. Quickly, Balian grabs the sword from the floor, holding it towards the approaching creatures. Across the road, the wolf from moments before lopes into view, bearing his teeth a long guttural howl escapes from his throat. Mariale and Balian can hear many answering howls from deep within the medieval forest.

The Silvery grey beast pads silently up to the entrance of the small cave. Never taking its' eyes from Balian. Growling, he warily enters the cave. Balian pushes Mariale behind him, shielding her from the beast. Balian slowly brings his small sword to bear against the Wolf, knowing it is little protection from a monster as this. Balian scream at the creature while it simple stands there looking at him. With a sudden rush, the wolf attacks Balian.

He swings the sword toward the beast, knowing it is late to stop its attack. He feels a giant weight hit his chest as the world explodes in flashes of light. Teeth tear into his shoulder, sending pain careening through his body. Balian feels blood flowing down his chest as he smells wet fur in his nostrils. Balian feels pressure and pain ripping through his shoulder as he cries out in agony. His vision begins to dim. Suddenly, the weight is off him as the wolf jumps back.

Hiding in the back of the cave, Mariale shrinks away at the sight of the wolf loping into the cave. The sight of its red glowing eyes frightens her. As the wolf jumps at Balian she steels herself, jumping at the great wolf she pounds it on the side of the head, it doesn't seem to notice her at all. In the corner of her eye she sees a figure come into view as she repeatedly strikes at the beast. Looking at the figure she sees that a nomad from the northern forest firing an arrow from his great bow. With a howl of pain the wolf jumps back, losing its hold on Balian. Taking a single bound the silver wolf is gone into the night.

Looking at the figure silhouetted in the dark entrance, he silently points to Balian, quickly moving out the cave disappearing into the dark night. Rushing to Balian, Mariale pulls his shirt away from the wound. Blood is freely flowing from it in streams. Rushing to the back of the cave, she grabs the small bag that Nellian gave her. Pulling a little pouch out, Mariale pushes some herb into the wound; taking a cloth she puts pressure against his shoulder. Looking down at Balian she silently prays that she can heal him. Taking long strips of cloth she binds the wound tightly.

A sound pulls her attention to the front of the cave. Standing in the entrance is one of the nomads from the forest. He silently walks up to Balian lying on the ground. Swiftly he picks him up. Looking at Mariale he walks out of the cave. Quickly Mariale follows him out of the cave. Following a trail along the hill they enter a cave behind the small cave facing the road.

The nomad silently lays Balian on the floor, turning to the entrance he leaves without a word. Looking around, the cave, Mariale sits next to Balian, pulling up his shirt she sees the bleeding has stopped. Feeling his skin, she is shocked that it feels warm to the touch already. Quickly, Mariale pulls a small basket out of her bag, taking little globes of light she places them around the cave. Quickly she feels the warmth of the globes reach her. Pulling Balian to the back of the cave, she cradles his head in her lap stoking his hair with her hand.

Slowly, the images of the attack come to her mind. Sometime during the night, she falls asleep, dreaming of days that they are walking among the fields quietly talking. Mariale wakes from the heat coming from Balians brow, she feels as if her hand is on fire. Jerking her eyes open she pulls her hand away from his brow, almost immediately feeling guilty. Even with her hand a foot away she can feel the heat emanating from him. Unable to stand it she quickly moves from underneath him. Lying on the ground he is moaning in agony. Tossing and turning, he seems almost on fire. Marialefrantically searches through the bag Nellian gave her, unable to find anything that could remotely help him, she is cursed to sit there helpless. She can't even come within a few feet of him. All day and night he hangs on, the fever flowing and ebbing. Sometimes he is too hot to approach, others he is ice cold. Hours after she woke, she sees a red baleful light coming from behind Balian eyes. Looking closer, she sees a glow coming from behind his eyelids. Small wisps of smoke lightly waft up to the cavern roof. As Mariale looks on, his muscles jerk with spasms. With a violent jerk, his back seems to almost break into two as he arches himself off the floor, just his toes and head holding him up off the ground. "Balian, come back to me, Balian!" Mariale wails in the long dreadful night. Unable to stand it any longer, Mariale passes out slumping to the ground.

Dreaming throughout the night, Mariale imagines a wolf loping up to her, as she sleeps. Slowly opening her eyes, she sees Baliantransformed into a ghastly red eyed beast. He looks down at her, his tongue lolling out of his mouth. His ears pricking up at a sound, he bounds out of the cave into the forest.

Hours later Mariale wakes. Balian is laying on the cave floor covered in bruises and blood. Jumping up Mariale hurries over to Balian, slowly reaching out to him, he is cool to the touch. Looking at him in the light of the glows she can't see one cut on him. Shrinking away, Mariale remembers the dream from last night. Balians eyelids start to blink. A flicker of red shines out from his eyes before he opens them, in amazement she sees his eyes are the palest blue she has ever seen. Pulling her knees up to her chest, she gently rocks back against the wall, not moving.

Pulling himself up from his back, Balian sits up with a groan. Memories of last night flood back to his shattered mind. Griping his head in his hands he groans and falls back to the floor. Instinctively, Mariale jumps up from the floor, rushing over to Balian. "Balian, what's wrong?" Opening his eyes, she sees immense pain flowing from them. "Balian, What's wrong, why are you hurting, your shoulder is already healed?" Mariales cries to him. "Mariale I feel like my insides are boiling. I can't take it!" Rolling over on to his back, Balian arches his body like last night. Screaming in agony, he collapses on the floor, unconscious.

Throughout the next few days Balian drifts in and out of nightmares, his body fluctuating from boiling hot to ice cold. Mariale sits his side, quietly bearing his torment. On the morning of the fifth day since the attack, Balian sits up after a long quiet night. Slowly stretching, he stands up. Balian feels as he is reborn, he feels his vision sharper. From outside in the distance he can hear birds chirping, not just one, but many from miles away. In amazement even being miles away he can smell the salty ocean air. His senses are assaulted with smell coming from everywhere. Looking at Mariale, he can feel her apprehension as she looks at him, he walks slowly to her. With a comforting smile he holds his arms out to her; she buries her head in his shoulder, softly crying. After some time he takes her by the hand leading her back out into the light of day.

In the distance he can smell the odor of soldier approaching. The smell of their fear leaves a pall over the forest, "Mariale, gather our things we need to get moving." Mariale quickly gathers their possessions together. Leading the way out of the cave, they start heading east. Stopping for a moment, Balian comes across a familiar scent. Looping back around to the side of the road, Balian can tell that Ran recently walked down it. Mingled among his smell are the smell of many Melcarens. He stops looking around, amazed at the many scents that abound in the world around him. Even the stream yards away, carries a strong scent. Looking at Mariale, he points down the road. "It's been a week or more Mariale, but he wasn't alone. With him went many Melcaren soldiers, He must have been captured." Looking back up the road, Balian hears a branch break some distance away. Prodding Mariale, he leads her down the road at a fast walk. Staring at him while they walk, Mariale isn't sure what to think of him now. The attack in the forest changed Balian; she just isn't sure in what way.

They walk along the forest road for hours, not seeing anyone. In the distance, they hear thunder booming. The smell of new rain is evident upon the wind. Soon they notice the trees are growing less. "Mariale, is the light getting brighter?" Balian asks as he looks up through the tree top. Mariale is taken back by his words. She quickly looks away from him, looking up at the trees. "I…I…think it is." Mariale responds to him. Confused, Balian looks around at her, "Mariale, What is wrong?" swaying slightly on her feet; she slowly looks at him timidly. "Balian, what happened the other night after you were attacked? So many things have happened, I just don't know who, or what you are now! That wound should of killed you, and then after."

Looking back into her eyes, Balian realizes that the last few weeks have been hard on her, maybe too hard. "Mariale, I am who I was before, I am just something more. The old me, is still here buried deep inside." Walking close to her, he takes her hand placing it on his chest. Feel my heart Mariale. It still beats; I'm just different now than before. Most of the time I feel the same, but I can smell and hear better than ever. I can't explain what happened, but, that is a part of me now. Please understand. I don't feel any different or think different."

Taking hold of him, she pulls him close, looking up she studies his eyes. "Your eyes are different now, but I can feel it is still you Balian." As they are standing there, Balian stiffens in her arms. "Balian, what is it?" Looking around he quickly relaxes. "I smelled Weldons on the breeze. That is odd out here." Quickly looking at the surrounding forest, Mariale pulls away from him. "Balian, let's get going, I want to find Ran." Pointing to the east they move off down the road. Soon, in the distance they can see a plain ahead. Lightning clashes in the sky south of them. The road winds among the low hills of the plain as the forest comes to an end. In the distance they can see two travellers upon the road. Balian, prods Mariale forward as the wind picks up, making it difficult to walk.

Moving into a small ravine below the crest of a hill, the winds slackens a bit. The thunder storm approaching drowns out all sound around them. As it rains harder rivulets of water starts flowing down the banks of the ravine, making the road slick under their feet. Slowly, they make their way to the top of the hill. A stroke of lightning comes down with feet of them, throwing them to the ground, Mariale screams in fright. Smelling the sulfur in the air, they quickly make it to the top of the ravine. As Balian crests the hill, he feels a dagger point pressed against his throat. Close to his ear he hears a voice, "Don't move boy!" In front of him, Mariale is on her knees looking up at Feal. Her hand is engulfed in a blue glow. Balian knows with one wrong move, that Feal will strike Mariale.

A deep guttural growl erupts from Balians throat as Derhuick presses the dagger harder. "I said don't move, you little whelp or your friend dies, Now get up and slowly walk." Quickly releasing Balian, Derhuick pulls a slender sword, jabbing it into his back. Feal, steps back, keeping her hand pointed at Mariale. "Walk, down the road boy, and stay calm! Mariale move to Balians side."

Following the road a short distance, Derhuick motions toward the north, "start walking that way Balian, and don't forget what I said." Walking over a small hill, Balian can see a small ruin of a castle in the distance. Looking back, he can see Feal, still ready to strike, 'he could take Derhuick, he is sure but, Feal is another matter." Looking at Mariale, he sees her resigned expression. Silently he swears that they will get away. The storm is raging as the come up to the ruins. Derhuick prods Balian ahead down a stair case leading into the darkness below them. Small white lights guide them below. At the bottom of the stairs, they enter a large barren room. Looking back, they see a door. They are lead farther into the ruins. Coming into a second room farther back, Derhuick points to chairs set against the back wall. Motioning to them they are forced to sit. "Well now, we caught up to atleast two of you," Derhuick growls. With Feal standing to the side, they are tightly bound to the chairs with ropes. Looking at them Derhuick questions them. "Alright you two, we have had a long chase, tell me where your friend is! We know he is around here somewhere. Where is he?'

Looking at Derhuick, Balian responds, "Why should we tell you, you want to kill him?" Glancing to Feal, Derhuick grins, "Because boy, if you don't tell me, you and your friend will meet a bad end here, now tell me!"

Looking up at Derhuick, Balian smiles, "We will not betray Ran." Feal moves forward slowly looking at Balian. "What has happened to your eyes?" she asks him. When Balian doesn't answer Feal walks over to Mariale, a red glow surrounds her hand, with a sickening thud Mariale is thrown back against the wall, a red glow burning a hole through her shirt. Balian can smell the scent of burnt cloth and flesh as Mariale screams in pain. Pulling at the ropes binding him, Balian attempts to stand, his muscles straining. Derhuick takes a step back as Balians' eyes flare a deep red. Stopping her attack on Mariale, Feal turns back to Balian, "What has happened to you Balian? I feel old magic flowing through your veins."

Balian strains at his bonds, unable to break them, he looks up at Feal glaring. "I swear if you don't let her be I will kill you." A deep guttural growl escapes his throat; instinctively Derhuick and Feal take a step backwards at the sound. Feal and Derhuick exchange worried glances. Looking closer at Balian, Feal notices a shimmering silver nimbus surrounding him. "Derhuick, I think we might want to leave for a while." Feal, nervously glances backwards at the door.

"Leave for what reason, I came a long way to track down these little whelps." Derhuick responds to Feal. Derhuick turns to Feal in time to see her disappearing up the stairway. As he turns back to Balian, he sees a red glowing light emanating from behind Balians eyelids. "What by the ancestors are you doing, Boy?" Derhuick sees a shimmering silvery light begin to envelope Balian. Derhuick slowly takes a step backwards toward the stairs unable to take his eyes off of the sight in front of him. Balian's bonds slip away as he transforms into a silvery grey wolf, standing easily five feet at the shoulders. Derhuick silently prays as the wolf looks eye to eye with him. Its muzzle curling back showing large fangs, a deep primeval growl filling the small room, knowing it is too late; Derhuick turns to flee as Balian launches himself at Derhuick. In a blur of motion, Derhuick is lying on the floor with his throat torn out. Fleeing for her life down the road, Feal almost sobs with fear, a primeval howl from ages long past splits the night. Fleeing across the hilly plains, Feal looks back seeing the silver wolf gaining on her. In the darkness of the night Feal doesn't see the small drop off until she is upon it. With a gasp, she plummets down the bank landing heavily; the last thing she remembers before darkness overtakes her is looking up in the sky seeing a large eagle pass over.

Balian slows his pursuit, looking up in the sky he sees a large hawk circling in the night sky. Somehow it feels familiar, without knowing why he stops his pursuit, turning back to the ruins and Mariale. Within minutes Balian is approaching the ruins, swiftly he changes forms before hurrying down the stairs to Mariale. Balian enters the room seeing Mariale struggling against her bonds. Quickly her cuts her bonds helping her from the chair, "Are you ok, Mariale?" rubbing her arms Mariale responds, "Yes, I think so, though my arms are sore, what happened to Feal Balian?"

Looking back up the stairs he answers her, "I'm not sure, I was running to catch her and as a hawk flew past I lost the will to chase her. It was funny, like I knew it, I don't understand it. I just felt this overwhelming need to get back here." Looking closely at her, he could see she was still scared. "What do you say about getting out of here?" Balian asks her.

Chapter Twelve
The Weldonsx

An ancient spirit walks the castle halls. Dead Weldons litter the corridors. Once again, Meroth is home. Ages have passed since the Weldons invaded their lands. 'Revenge is sweet' thinks Meroth. Movement out of the corner of his eye catches his attention, in the corner of a recess in the hall, a Weldon man stares at him. As Meroth stops, the man tries to flee down the hall. Almost as if the man was a flea, Meroth points at him. Instantly the man is thrown against the wall with a bone splintering crunch.

Coming to the end of the hall, Meroth walks down the stairs out into the inner courtyard of the castle. Groups of Turiec are gathered near the eastern wall. He sees that the gate is barred from the other side. Calmly walking over, he motions for the captain. "What is this captain?" He demands. Pointing back to the gate he responds, "Meroth, the Weldons have barred the eastern gate, we are attempting to break through now."

Without acknowledging his words, Meroth motions for his people to move away. As the Turiec move back from the gate, Meroth unsheathes his sword. Blue flames snake along the black blade as he walks toward the gate. Coming closer to the gate, the runes on his armor start to shimmer and ebb in a blue glow. The very air crackles as he speaks a command in an ancient language. Pointing his sword at the gate, a great rending sound is heard in the courtyard. The gate starts to vibrate as the stone of the gate, begins to crack. Within seconds, cracks begin to radiate out from the center. In an ear shattering explosion, the gate explodes inward toward the Weldons.

With a shout of triumph the Turiec burst down through the gate, striking down all remaining Weldons where they stand stunned. With his voice booming above all in the courtyard, he commands his people, "Follow and hunt down all of them, leave none alive!" Turning around, Meroth proceeds towards the western side of the castle. The sights of battle are everywhere, Weldon corpses lay everywhere.

Walking to the southwestern courtyard, Meroth sees the well in the center of the courtyard. Remembering the castle all too well, he strides through a small door in the western wall. Walking down a small hallway, Meroth comes to a wide staircase at the end of the corridor. Quickly striding up the stairs, he follows it as it opens into a great throne room. Stopping in the entrance, he looks around the room. 'Ages have passed since he was here' he silently thinks. Feeling a familiar presence he slowly makes his way into the center of the room. A high arched ceiling fades into the darkness, while surrounding the room; statues of Turiec warriors silently wait the passage of time. Meroth looks at the throne in the center of the room on a raised dais. High backed with runes engraved on its surface, with a word they began to shimmer in the cold air. Seeing a flicker of movement out of the corner of his eye he silently ignores it. 'Let him see the end of his people' he thinks. With a wave of his hand bright white light illuminates the room. Meroth slowly walks around the room studying the statues. Thirty statues silently stand vigil in his throne room these past ages. Each one is wearing black armor, intricately engraved with ancient runes. Great swords hang from their backs in silver sheaths. Smiling, he slowly walks to the throne near the back of the room. Looking down at it, the runes are ebbing with power.

Turning around he looks at the door at the other side of the room. "Roanoled, you can quit skulking and show yourself." Meroth speaks to the empty air. At the other end of the throne room, a white light begins to shimmer and shift in the air. A figure in golden armor appears from the shimmering light. "Meroth, you do not belong here, your time is over." The ghost of the king speaks.

With a hollow laugh Meroth looks on the old king, "Your people flee for their lives, I am back from the cold dead north Roanoled, you or no one else can stop me!" Seeming to float across the floor, the old king comes up to Meroth looking intently at his face. "You were always arrogant Meroth; The High king is alive again." King Roanoled responds. With a smile Meroth answers, "Your boy king shall be dead soon, just as your people are dying this moment, now go from my sight, your time ended long ago. My rein has begun again." Slowly King Roanoled starts fading from sight. "Ranwulf will triumph in the end Meroth."

Meroth speaking to the empty air slowly responds, "We shall see king of a dead country, we shall see." Looking around the room his voice cracking through the air he summons his soldiers, "My faithful Solarus, come back to me know, Wake and serve me!" Slowly the runes on the statues armor flicker, steadily growing brighter and stronger. Meroth slowly sits down on his throne as each of the statues begins to come alive. Power emanates from the runes engraved upon their armor, with slow faltering steps they move away from the walls. The Guardians' cross the room kneeling in front of Meroth. As one, they lay their swords on the ground, bowing to their king.

"Rise and serve me as in the ancient past my children, our time has come again, let us go out into the world again." With a great cry they raise their swords skyward. Swiftly rising from his throne, He draws his sword, lightning rippling along the blade. Streaming from the Throne room, they move swiftly through the castle chasing the fleeing Weldons to the eastern cities.Meroth followed by the Solarus stream through the eastern gateway, a black cloud of death moving towards the Weldon cities.

Through the night the Turiec make their way across the mountains towards Heriol. Black clouds race over the mountain, lightning striking the peaks as the army approaches the Weldon city. Meroth crests the last pass to Heriol. Standing in front of his people Meroth surveys the Weldon stronghold. Tall granite walls rise from the mountainside. Weldon figures are carved into the city walls, over the years they have been entombed in thick layers of ice, making the walls smooth. He looks at the walls, trying to find a weakness to exploit. The granite walls are easily twenty feet thick at the battlement without an opening in them. At the bottom is a small entrance the size of a door. The road follows the cliff edge around until it ends at a flowing bridge thirty feet long, crossing a deep chasm it is slender and graceful, being wide enough for just one at a time. Meroth looks to the top of the wall, seeing a robed figure staring back, he smiles a wickedly cruel smile. Turning around to the Solarus he commands them to follow. Striding slowly down the road, they unsheathe their long black swords as the snow begins to fall.

Upon the city walls Telenor, one of the last council members, stares out over the battlement at the approaching Turiec army. Turning to the captain of the city guard she asks him, "Captain, how is the evacuation proceeding?" Turning to her he responds, "Councilor Telenor, most of the women and children have left with the scouts, on your signal we will commence with the remainder of the people." Turning back to the approaching army, Telenor sees Meroth striding down the road followed closely by a squad of black armored figures. A chill ripples down her spine as a light snow begins to fall. "Captain, defend the city," she commands.

Spurring his men into action, they form two solid lines on the battlements overlooking the approaching figures. Weldons dressed in white fur carrying long bows made out of ice. As one they pull flickering blue arrows from their quivers. With a command from their captain, the fire as one at Meroth and the Solarus, hundreds of shimmering arrows fly towards them. Meroth stops, looking up at the cascade of arrows arching towards them. Silently they stand seemingly oblivious to the rain of arrows. As the arrows reach Meroth they shatter upon an invisible barrier, each one harmlessly disappearing into nothingness. Meroth begins chanting in a strange language. The Weldons can hear just a whisper upon the winds as they stand there waiting for the Turiec onslaught. Looking around they wonder what they hear on the wind. A chill beyond the cold seems to grow upon the wind. Voices echo off the valleys and cliffs, alien to hear. Looking around, Telenor feels the ancient ebb and flow of voices long gone. Voices being called upon once more, she feels a scream building up inside of her as she looks around seeing the panic on the Weldons faces. Grabbing the edge of the wall she peers down at Meroth, seeing him chanting words of power.

Summoning all the strength she has, she blocks out the wailing and screams around her, raising her arms to the sky. As she stands there staring into the heavens, a brilliant white light penetrates the black foreboding storm clouds, the Turiec flee from the intense light. The only ones left standing in place is Meroth, and his Solarus, while all others turn away from the city. Moving her hands in quick strange patterns the small point of light begins to grow, moving along the wall on either side of her. Instantly where it touches the ice it melts unleashing a flow of water over the city walls. Quickly mover over the walls the water quickly turns into a river, ripping the ice off the walls in a great torrent. Cascading down the walls the ice flows out over the chasm, with a great rush it flows up the mountain road straight at the Turiec army. The river of rock, ice and water surges up the road quickly closing the distance to the invading army. As it reaches Meroth it is split in two. Rushing past him it washes over the front of the Turiec. Great waves come crashing down on them, screams of panic and dismay can be heard over the thundering roar of the river. Hundreds of the Turiec are washed off the road down high cliffs. In the middle of it Meroth stands in an island untouched.

As quickly as the onslaught began it is over, leaving the Turiec army floundering on the mountainside. Telenor standing on the city walls looks down, seeing the destruction she wrought upon them. Great slabs of the road had been washed away to fall down into the canyon below. Surveying the damage she had done, she noticed a grey spot in her eyesight. Calling the captain over to her, she points, "What do you make of it captain?" Looking down squinting he points at Meroth and his Solarus. I think it's coming from behind them. Its' beyond me to know what it is, never seen such a thing in my life." Looking down upon the road they can see a grey mist forming around the figures in the road. Seeming in the midst of it they can see small flickers of orange fire. As it passes over Meroth his chanting grow heavy and rhythmic. The mist starts to turn black at the edges slowly moving inward as it gets closer. The closer it comes to the city the higher it floats, growing larger by the second.

"Captain, get all your men off the wall." Without a word he commands them to retreat below the inner wall. Telenor stands there waiting for the attack. Closing the distance by half the cloud is almost completely black with flickering orange flames floating around inside it. It is now wider than the wall, growing taller by the moment. Telenor takes her staff spinning it in circles, while runes of blue and white flow out of the ends, quickly turning into a white wispy cloud spinning fast. With a command the cloud shoots toward the figures on the ground. Striking a barrier, just in front of the Solarus it spins around it, seeking a place to break through. Still flowing from her staff it takes shape and form of a Weldon figure. The cloud dancing against the barrier, it finds a small weakness in the layer of protection. Striking again and again in moments, it breaks through with a deafening howl of wind and rain into the inner barrier of Meroth. With the power of a hurricane it whips Meroth to the ground, throwing the Solarus into chaos. Seeking the closest Solarus it envelopes it in a gale of power, lifting it up into the air, the cloud flings it out over the cliff and far down into the valley below.

In triumph Telenor looks to see the confusion of her enemy as she prepares for another attack. Looking overhead she sees the black cloud floating over the city walls. Orange flames rage inside it. In horror she sees a small drop of orange fire drops from the cloud. As it touches the wall, flames leap up flowing away from it in an oily puddle. Where ever it touches the rock smokes. In horror she sees the rock begin to melt where it touches the top of the wall. Bubbles form as it slowly melts its way through the stone as if it was ice, quickly looking around she sees the orange flame trickling onto the wall everywhere underneath the cloud. Understanding that it is just a matter of time before the wall falls, she runs to the stairs calling for the captain. Seeing him below her on the lower parapet she hurries over to him, "Captain, we can't hold the wall any longer, we must evacuate everyone out of the city."

While the outer wall starts to weaken from the onslaught of the fire, the Weldons race to leave. Streaming out of the eastern gate, Telenor is the last to leave. Looking back as the western wall falls she is thrown to the ground as it bucks and heaves from the collapse. Scrambling back to her feet she hurries away east, as the Turiec army pour through the gaps in the fallen wall. Following the road up away from the city, Telenor catches up with the stragglers fleeing the city. Looking out over the mountains Telenor sees darkness falling upon the mountains as black rolling clouds moved southward over the mountains. Lightning flashes in the distance, striking the tops of in branching forks as thunder booms in the distance. Coming around a curve in the road she sees the road has partially washed away as they are slowed to a crawl, going around the curve in single file. After everyone has moved away, just her and a few soldiers stand at the curve looking back. "We can't hold them here, but maybe we can slow them down a little" she tells them. Bringing her staff to bear, a rune flares to life, flying from the end of it as it speeds towards the washed out road. As it closes the distance, it forms into a small ball of light; with a great thump it strikes the cliff just below the road, spraying them with clots of earth and rock. Looking on, they hear a crack and feel a shutter in the ground as a great slab of the cliff breaks free, the road disappearing down the cliff.

Looking at the fallen road, Telenor urges the Weldons on "We must hurry and make as much distance as we can tonight, for the Turiec will not be stopped by that, just slowed down." Streaming through the mountains are the remnants of a once proud and powerful people, their leader scattered or dead. Telenor know she will have to lead her people into the southern lands and somehow keep them alive. Thinking to herself, she knows the Turiec will not stop until they have destroyed every one of them. Throughout the night she pushes them onward through the passes and canyons of the mountains.

For two days Telenor pushes the Weldons through the mountains. Every settlement they have passed has been deserted, showing signs of her people fleeing to the east. As the morning of the third day approaches the Weldons find themselves on a pass overlooking the forests to the south. In the distance she sees thousands of Weldons making their way down different paths to the forest below. Turning to the captain she tells him, "Captain, we need to get down to the forest as soon as we can." Silently looking at the mountains they choose a small narrow path close to the one they are on, quickly the captain taking the lead, they follow it down. Throughout the morning they make their way down the path, making the first of the trees above the forest mid-day. Farther down the hillside Telenor can see many Weldons gathered. "Captain, down there," she says pointing at the groups below. Following the path down the hillside they reach the Weldons near the bottom in short time.

Searching for any familiar faces among the group she sees none, silently wondering who is left from the destruction of Nerost. As she approaches them, the Weldons start to gather around her, all of them shouting questions and demanding she tell them what is happening. Holding her hands up to them she motions for them to be quiet. "Quiet everyone, listen and I will tell you what I can." With her words they Weldons quickly stop talking as the rest move in closer. "My people, we have been invaded by an ancient enemy, our cities are gone, or very soon will be. It is only a matter of time, before they find the way we came out of the mountains. We need to get moving and head into the southern forests. Our cities may be gone, but we survive." Looking around at the faces staring at her, she asks them."

157

"Is there anyone here from Nerost, as anyone seen any of the council?" A voice farther in answers her. "Council woman, I was at Thurgel before we evacuated. I overheard one of the council members talking about heading east to warn the other cities."

Taking in the information, Telenor looks around at the Weldons gathered around her. "I don't know what is to become of us yet, but we need to keep moving. The best thing we can do is head south into the forests and hopefully our enemy won't follow us so far south. I have to guess that most of our people that survive will be heading south too. With any luck, we should be able to find them there." Turning around she looks at the captain, "Captain, I want you and some others to stay and send any more Weldons after us when they come out of the mountains." Nodding at her he agrees, "Yes council member, I will do as you ask, if we see the Turiec we will send word to you." Turning back to the group she tells them. "Everyone, I will lead you south, all the women and children sty closer to the middle. All the soldiers form a perimeter around us; I don't know what we will find down there." She says pointing to the forests, "But, it probably won't take kindly to so many of us coming through, we will find a place to defend ourselves and wait for the others." The Weldon start to organize the group as ordered, while Telenor moves to the front. With a wave to the captain, she looks around the Weldon people wondering how she is going to keep them alive. A soldier walks up to her, offering to help her. "Council member, I am Hurite of the fifth house of Thurgel, how can my men and I be of service?" With a thankful expression she responds to him, "Hurite, can you help me find a good path down through the forests and give us warning of what's up ahead?"

"Consider it done Council member," he says. "Please Hurite, just Telenor, the council is gone."

Bowing his head to her he agrees, "Yes, Telenor." Turning away he quickly sends out thirty men to scout the path down, while he leads Telenor and the rest of the Weldons south. Looking back she sees more Weldons have joined bringing the total to atleast a thousand. Moving down the mountain side she sees more trees sprouting up and tuffs of grass growing. As the morning wears on, they start to enter the outer edge of the forest, as it gets more difficult to move from the brush and trees. Silently she thinks if the Turiec do follow them south it will be easy to find them. Already they are leaving a great open swathe of beaten down vegetation as they move through the edges of the forest. Hurite walking back to her tells her, "Telenor, we see no signs of anything Turiec or anything in front of us, though we sees a lot of strange prints in the ground, great large prints with many toes and claws, not sure what they belong to but, we have to be careful." Nodding to him she starts off once again. As the day wears on, she looks back over the group, seeing they are getting squeezed into a few thin lines winding through the forest. Seeing the sun nearing the horizon she decides they have to stop for the night, so everyone can rest a little. "Hurite, let's stop here and make camp for the night. Form a perimeter and start making a clearing large enough for everyone, use whoever you need, but make it quick and big enough for everyone." Waving to his men, they gather around him, "Men, we are going to stop here for the night, grab who you need and lets clear an area wide enough for everyone and set up a perimeter big enough for fires around it." With haste they each grab groups of men heading in different sides of the Weldons. In minutes the sound of axes and falling trees can be heard all around. Soon great fires are lit on the perimeter of the Weldons illuminating the forest in the dying light. Slowly as the night wears on, Weldons stream through the forest from the mountains to join them.

Sitting on a hastily thrown together platform, Hurite and her are talking, gathered around them are leading of the some of the households to escape death. Feriot of the twenty first house of Thurgel asks Telenor a question, "Telenor, what is your idea on where we should go and what should we do, the southern nations are not going to welcome us with open arms." Glancing around at the leaders gathered she tells them, "Well, to begin with, so everyone knows. The council is no more, I saw Melcore overcome by Meroth on the walls of Nerost. The rest as far as I know are dead or scattered across the mountains. In time maybe we will form a new council, but for now if we are to survive, all of the leaders of their house will have to take an active role in what we do and where we go from here. I suggest we head farther into the forest and set up a city to defend ourselves. We need to create a place that the scattered Weldons go make for."

Shouts of aye and yes can be heard around the meeting; Hurite stands up to be seen by everyone. "Unless anyone has any objections I will lead the scouts and fighting force." Looking around no one objects. "I have two hundred soldiers form the fifth house to defend us with. I need each one of you to send me half of your soldiers to me so we can organize our fighting troops." When everyone agrees Hurite sits down and Feriot stands up, looking at Telenor he says, "Now we atleast have a plan, let us meet every night so we can plan for the next day." Agreeing Telenor looks around, "I am going to walk around and see how everyone is doing, if anyone needs anything come find me, and I think it would be a good idea to stay here for tomorrow unless we see the turiec approaching from the mountains." With nods of agreement the group breaks up, Hurite and Telenor start making their way around the Weldons.

Walking along the perimeter, they see the Weldons have swelled through the day. Soldiers are busy, on the outskirts of the clearing cutting down more trees and expanding the ever widening perimeter. As they stand there looking at exhausted Weldons they hear a deep guttural howl from the forest. Quickly looking in the direction they see a great pair of eyes staring back at them from the dark forest. They can see a huge shambling form moving towards them from out of the forest. With a cry of surprise, Hurite orders Telenor protected. Quickly his men surround her. A squad of soldiers moves forward between them and the creature. Hurite looks on with horror when what looks like a shaggy tree moves into the light of the fires. Standing easily fifteen feet tall it is covered it thick matted brown hair, two red shining eyes stares out behind a fanged tooth mouth. Stopping right inside the hastily made clearing it, stands there looking back at them.

Hurite forms his men into a phalanx as they unsheathe their swords. The creature, stand there momentarily, then without warning, it brings its arms up in a gestures. Blue energy crackles along its' lower arms moving down towards its' fingertips. Telenor, seeing the magic flowing along its' arms instantly bring a shield up between her and it. With a snarl, the creature throws out ribbons of crackling energy at Telenor. Bouncing off her shield, it flows to the side, instantly knocking five Weldons to the ground. Smoke rises from their bodies as they convulse. With a yell, Hurite launches himself towards the creature, his battle-axe swinging through the air. Telenor lowers her shield, as white waves of energy flows from her to smite the creature in the chest. Stunned it stands there in place howling in rage and pain. With a battle cry Hurite strike with his battle-axe cleaving the creature in the middle of the chest, great gouts of blood spray from the wound, as it instinctively swings a first at

Hurite, knocking him away before it crumples on the ground. The forward squad of soldiers' moves forward hacking at the beast to insure it dies.

Shakily Hurite staggers back to his feet. Walking towards the creature he sees it is dead. Taking his axe from the creatures' chest he cleans it on the ground. Looking up as Telenor walks up he asks her, "How many more of those things do you think are out there?" Looking out at the dark forest she responds, "I hope not many, but something tells me I am wrong, we move into a dangerous world Hurite, and let's double the guard at once.Are you ok Hurite, you got hit pretty hard?' Turning to her with a slight smile, "I'm fine Telenor; it takes a lot more than that to kill me." The Weldons make a solid ring of guards around the perimeter, fencing themselves in from the denizens of the forest. Nothing else attacks them that night, though in the morning Telenor and Hurite see many tracks inside the forest as they look at the body of the dead creature. "What is it, Telenor?' Staring as the creature, she is forced to cover her mouth from the stench of it; they walk farther into the edge of the forest looking around the ground, trying to see what direction it came from. "I don't know what it is, but it looks like it came up from the south. I fear we will meet many more of them as we travel. How many Weldons have joined us, so far Hurite?" Pulling out a scroll he looks at it before answering her, "So far we have gathered a couplethousand of our people together, a far cry from how many were living in Thurgel, Telenor."

Walking back towards their people she tells him, "Well, good or bad, atleast we have managed to gather that many together make sure everyone gets rest today and we are leaving at first light in the morning, maybe if we wait today we can add more Weldons to our number." With a quick salute, Hurite moves away, leaving Telenor to ponder their next move.

Chapter Thirteen
The Southern Country

Bending over the rail yet one more time, Ran didn't think he had anything left in his stomach. He hurries away from the rail before the captain sees him. Grabbing a cool of rope he starts to climb up the forward mast. For the last two days he's been learning his way around the ship, the captain being a hard but fair taskmaster. He had learned to count time by the rhythm of waves slapping the prow of the ship. He had been silently amazed looking at his arms in the sun, now understanding that he had tanned quickly in the southern sun. He had felt that it was a matter of time before someone brought up his white skin, when one day he had looked at his arms and noticed he was the same deep tan as everyone around him.

A shout in the rigging overhead brings his attention to the front of the ship "Land Ho Captain, southeast" a sailor calls down. Hurrying to tie off the forward upper sail, before climbing down Ran looks out seeing a sight he would never imagined possible. For, out in the distance a hundreds of gleaming silver spires reach for the heaven. In the late evening sun, the horizon seems lit with silver fire. Ran hears a voice below him. "Boy, come down here." Looking down he sees Antonius standing there. Climbing down, Ran hurries up to him. Pointing at the horizon, Antonius tells him, "That Ran is Berius, the city of silver. For all the buildings are clad in a layer of silver." Walking towards the bow, Antonius takes Ran in tow. "Ran, when we arrive at Berius, stay close to my side and speak to no one, unless I instruct you to first, we will be starting your training in earnest once we leave Berius and start inland towards Melcar. I will be leading a large force back to the capital in time for the winter celebrations."

Looking down at Ran, Antonius puts his hand on his shoulder looking, back out over the horizon "isn't that a sight to behold Ran?" Looking at the silver city, Ran feels a wave of nausea threaten to overwhelm him. He fled from one enemy headlong into another with no way to escape. Misunderstanding his reaction Antonius nods his head, "Yes, Ran it can be overwhelming."

Standing at the rail with Antonius, they watch as the crew deftly brings the ship through the breakwaters heading into port. As Ran looks on, he slowly realizes the enormity of the Melcaren people. Hundreds of warships are anchored in the bay before the docks. Ran has never seen so many people. Berius was a hive of activity with thousands crawling along the docks. Wagons were moving in all directions, with brightly colored soldiers in sight everywhere. With a quick practiced ease the captain moves the ship through the tightly packed bay, docking it in a short time. As soon as the gangplank was lowered, a man in silver plate armor boards. Antonius seeing the man went to attention, saluting him with a quick snap of his fist.

"Antonius, you are to report to the citadel immediately, the northern territories are in turmoil." The soldier tells Antonius. "Yes commander" without waiting for a response the soldier disappears down the gangplank back into the bustle of activity on the docks. 'Let's go Ran, and remember do not say a word unless I tell you to first." Quickly Antonius and Ran make their way down to the dock, moving towards the towers in the distance. As they move through the crowd, everyone makes way for them, a small sea of calm in an ocean of activity. Looking around, Ran sees a city bursting from the seams with people. Trailing Antonius, Ran is assaulted by the smells and sights of a true southern city. The streets are paved with white flag stones. The buildings are a muted grey down here by the docks, but as they approach farther in, he sees yellows and gold buildings with brass or copper roofs. Everyone he sees is dressed in brightly colored pantaloons and loose fitting flowing shirts. For the heat is stifling among all the people. Without realizing it, as they turned a corner, Ran caught a glimpse of the harbor far below. They had climbed up without knowing it. Coming around the corner, they are met by a small squad of soldier.

The soldier in the lead quickly salutes him, falling into step next to him. "Antonius I was sent to escort you quickly to the commander." The soldier tells him. "What is happening cerlio?" Antonius asks him. "Antonius, I was explicitly told to ask you to wait for any explanation until the commander could talk to you."

Nodding quickly at Cerlio, Antonius quickens his pace. Coming around a building Ran looks up to see a lofty city wall coming into view. Even higher than the walls at home in the north, as they pass through the city gate, Ran is stunned by the sight in front of him. Immense spires snake toward the sky. Each one is a hundreds of yards across and seems to touch the sky. He almost falls backwards trying to see to the top of one. They are painted brightly in many different colors. With the tops of them shining even in the dim light, the streets are lit with lanterns. While light spills from windows of the buildings, inside the inner city, Ran sees only soldiers.

They walk through the inner city quickly, soldiers stopping and saluting as they pass. Coming around a corner of a spire, they walk into a wide parade ground. Poles with banners on them are set along the edges near the door to different buildings. In the center of the square is the largest spire Ran has seen yet. It seems to drive itself straight up to the sky. As they approach the spire, a man in white robes comes into view, he swiftly joins them, stepping up next to Antonius. "Commander Antonius, it is pleasant to see you back among us again."

"Verlium, it has been sometime since I was around the brotherhood," Antonius answers him, "Follow me, commander, the Great Priruit wishes to speak with you immediately." Almost missing a step Antonius glances at Verlium, "He is here, in Berius?" Without another word Verlium continues on to the archway leading into the center building in the square.

Walking inside Ran sees a great entrance room, paved in marble flagstones. Brightly colored tapestries line the walls, depicting epic battles. A line of soldiers surround the walls. Quickly they walk through the entrance room to a staircase farther back. It is easily twenty feet wide, slowly climbing the outer wall of the spire. Moving up a few floors, they come to an intricately carved arch, protected by a full squad of soldiers. Verlium, waves them to the side, quickly coming to an inner door in a smaller room. Verlium signals Antonius to follow him. Taking Ran in tow, the three enter the antechamber setup for the Great Priruit of the Melcaren people.

Ran sees a small old woman sitting at a table near the back of the richly decorated room. Broad tapestries of royalty ordain the walls. A large marble lit fireplace warms the room. Antonius and Verlium, instantly kneel before the Priruit, Ran following suite. "Stand Antonius, Verlium. Who is this young boy you bring today?" Looking back at Ran Antonius responds, "Great Priruit, this boy was found in Britannia by one of our patrols. He has been recruited into our cause and I have taken him to be my Freduit." Motioning for Ran to approach, she looks closely at his face. "I sense something in you boy. Listen well to Antonius and you shall have a bright future in our country." With a dismissive wave, Ran is sent to the side. Slowly standing from her chair the Priruit walks to the side window in the room looking out. Antonius and Verlium silently await her words.

Turning back to them she speaks slowly, "Antonius you are to take our full force from Melcar and go to the northeastern border. Our scouts tell me that the Weldons have been invaded by a force to their north. They are now fleeing through the eastern mountains. We must make sure they don't look south upon our lands." Feeling eyes on him Ran pretends to dispassionately stare at a tapestry in front of him, while inside he is panicking. 'His people, invaded, by whom he wonders, He darts a glance around the room his eyes being drawn to the frail old woman, who is now intently staring at him. He quickly lowers his eyes to the floor.

"Tell me Antonius was your search in vain again, did you find it?" the Priruit asks him. Looking at her, he responds quietly, "No, Priruit I have not found it, the sword still escapes us. In time we will find it." Walking towards the fireplace she calmly replies. "Antonius, events move in the world that we are not prepared for yet, we must find that sword if our people are to survive, it is in Britannia. For now, get the army to the northern border, train your Freduit to follow you, but as quickly as you can return to Britannia and find that sword."

Being dismissed they make their way back towards the outer city. Verlium parts ways with Antonius, "I will see you in the northern country Antonius. Travel well my old friend." Clasping hands they part for their own missions. Without a word, Antonius takes Ran in tow. Following the twisting and turning streets they walk to the outer city walls. Once, they approach the gates, Antonius calls out to the guards. "Soldier, bring me two fresh mounts fully stocked with provisions." His red and silver armor proclaiming his status in the army, the soldiers hurry away. Looking back at Ran, he seems on the point of saying something then thinks better of it. At that point the soldier come back with two horses, they quickly fill the saddlebags as Antonius impatiently waits.

Once, they are ready, Antonius mounts, while Ran struggles to gain the saddle. After a minute, Ran is mounted while Antonius takes the leads of Rans' horse; they start out of the city gates down the dusty road inland. Within a couplehours Ran feels like he has walked for a week. Looking down the road, Antonius brings the horses to a stop under a loan tree by the side of the road. Getting off his horse he motions for Ran to do the same. With his muscles cramping to the ground, Antonius tells him to walk the horses for a few minutes, then to feed them. Taking out a small bedroll Antonius lies down by the tree and is quickly asleep; leaving Ran to do what he is told. Looking out over the plains outside the city at night, Ran fleetingly thinks of fleeing, but then decides it would be easy for Antonius to catch him. Nor does he dare use magic here. Where would he go anyway?

In a blur of motion, Antonius comes off the ground, pummeling Ran in the face. In a heap Ran hits the ground. Instinctively he jumps back onto his feet, ready to fight or flee. "Lesson time, Ran" Antonius tells him. Walking in circles around each other they face off. Quicker than he thought possible, Antonius closes the distance between them, before he can strike Ran throws his full weight against Antonius bringing them both down to the ground in a heap. Antonius throws Ran off him, coming to his feet in an instant.

"Well Ran, you surprise me, your quick and know how to fight with your hands, do you know how to use a sword though?" Walking over to his horse, Antonius brings out two short swords. Throwing one to Ran, Antonius unsheathes it. Ran quickly unsheathes his, holding the sheath in his left hand. Knowing full well that Antonius will not wait, He approaches Antonius. Swinging the sword in a small arc, he hears the blades strike each other. With his left hand he jabs Antonius in the neck with its point. Satisfied with a grunt of acknowledgement, he backs up. In a flurry of movement Antonius charges Ran, with a quick thrust cut motion Antonius disarms Ran, leaving him holding an empty sheath. Staring at Antonius, he sees that he has his sword. The remainder of the night is filled with lessons. Shortly before dawn, Antonius relents, letting Ran lay on the ground and sleep. In the light of the moon, Antonius is pondering about his Freduit. He has skill in fighting, but will need many more lessons soon if he is to survive in the Melcaren army.

Through the week as they travel across the hills and plains of Melcaren, Antonius teaches Ran the art of fighting, by the time they are within a day of Melcar, Antonius is satisfied that Ran may survive for a little while. After a days' long ride, Ran is feeding the horses as they make camp for the night. Over the Horizon Ran sees a bright glow coming from the east. "Sir, what is that?" Looking gat the eastern sky Antonius responds, "That is the army waiting for us, Ran. We will be joining it in the morning. You will need your sleep tonight, so there will be no lessons tonight."

Breathing a silent sigh of relief, Ran finishes feeding the horses and lays down to sleep. Ran sleep is disturbed throughout the night with dreams of Weldons fleeing through the ice covered mountains. Wondering where his people will go, he tosses and turns all night. Sitting a few yards away, Antonius can see the boys sleep is troubled, probably dreaming about being at home instead of here he thinks. But, yet there is that nagging feeling that there is something about him that isn't right. Looking away he thinks of the past, 'probably getting too old for this sort of thing' thinks Antonius. Looking at the northern sky, Antonius sees a furious lightning storm heading south over the plains. Judging the distance, he figures the storm will be there in a couple hours. Walking over to Ran he prods him awake. "Ran, get up we need to make some miles before that storm makes it here." Quickly getting their things together Ran and Antonius saddle the horses and start down the road towards Melcar.

As they travel through the night, the glow in the east gets brighter. Shortly before dawn, Ran starts to make out a great camp out on the plains in front of them. He can see thousands of soldiers; behind the army is a host of wagons and horses. Sitting straighter in his saddle Antonius motion to the army in the distance, seeing a column of riders break off from the main camp coming there direction.

Antonius drills into him one more time, "Now, remember Ran, do not talk to anyone unless I instruct you to." Ran points to the south seeing movement on the open plain, "What is that, Sir?" Looking south, Antonius can't make out any detail. "I don't know, let's start moving faster." The horses pace picks up from a walk to a canter. Looking south they can tell the smudge is quickly moving north. They start to feel a pounding of hooves over the ground as the mass gets closer, to the east they see the column of soldiers pick up speed. With a shout Antonius spurs his horse toward the column. "Ran, get moving or it's our death!" Digging his heels into his horses flank, Ran gallops madly behind Antonius. Leaning over his horses' neck, he sees the mass evolve into a nightmarish sight. Coming from the south are hideous creatures from his nightmares. The creatures are tall, each one a blackish grey color, having long narrow scales like skin, yellow eyes look out from a feathered head. They each ride a scaly creature shaped like a horse, but easily twice the size.

Even with pushing their horses as hard as possible, the creatures seem to fly over the open plain. "Ran, draw your sword, they will make it to us before our soldiers do," Antonius calls back to him.

Pulling their horses up short, they stop and prepare for an impossible fight. Antonius points at the creatures fast approaching "They are called the Delium; they are creatures from the most southern plains. I have never heard of them this far north or mounting such a daring raid as this. When they are within a few hundred yards a bellow comes from the fore most Delium, a scream of rage that curdles Rans' stomach. Pulling long scimitars from their saddles, most of the Delium break away heading towards the column of horsemen approaching, that still leaves well over a hundred of them bearing down on them.

Panicked, Ran looks to Antonius. Watching him intently Antonius salutes him. "Ran, die bravely." With a spur of his horse Antonius is charging the beasts with his sword held aloft. Feeling death rapidly approaching, Ran retreats into his memories of his true father, Lord Roanoled. He remembers the words spoken a lifetime ago in the throne room below the castle. Time seems to slow down as Ran sees one of the Delium riding down on him. Its' scimitar aimed for his neck. Impulsively the red runes appear in his head, without thinking Ran picks one out, causing it to form in the air in front of him. The Delium widening his eyes as it sees the magic appears in front of the soldier.

Pointing his sword at the Delium, the red ruin b urs with motion, abruptly turning into a small fireball. Instantly the fireball shoots from the end of Rans' sword engulfing the creature in fire. Ran sees the Delium fall off its dead mount. A sharp bellow erupts from the creature as it dies. The Delium surprised, falter in their attack. Antonius spins around on his mount almost pitching over the side of it. Forgetting the rush of the Delium Antonius spurs his horse towards Ran, coming up from the back, a Delium slashes at Antonius, swinging widely hitting his mount. In a heap Antonius falls beneath his mount, unmoving.

Looking around, Ran sees nowhere to escape, a few yards away a Delium approaches him with his scimitar raised to strike. In a blur of motion, Ran forms another fireball quickly engulfing the creature in it. The remaining Delium turn to the east, understanding Ran is a foe beyond them. Looking east Ran sees the column of soldiers in locked battle with the Delium. Ran turns his horse west, spurring it into a gallop. The sounds of battle slowly dissolve into the distance as Ran flees. Panicking, he isn't sure which way to go, he is in the middle of the Melcaren nation, among enemies.

Keeping his horse in a gallop he quickly makes his way across the plains, the battle disappearing into the distance. Bringing his horse to a canter, Ran looks around, he must go somewhere that he can rest for a while. The world has gone mad around him. Mariale and Balian are back in Britannia with Nellian. If he went north maybe he could find the Weldons hiding in the forest. A rain drop spatters on his face. Looking north he sees the storm is almost upon him, he decides that north is the best choice for now until he can decide what to do. More rain comes down as the southern edge of the storm approaches. In the distance he sees lightning flashes and can hear the thunder rumbling. He has no idea how far the forest is but, better to start now than later.

Wrapping his cloak closer around him, he slowly makes his way north through the night as the storm rolls in. A short time before dawn, Ran sees he is drawing into an area of small hills, looking out over water filled gullies and small streams formed the night before. Getting down from his horse he lets the horse drink. Bending down next to the horse he fills his water flask, looking around he sees a small Range of mountains' to the west while the hills continue on northward. Looking at the mountains he thinks he could hide easier in them if spotted. He is slowly drying out from the drenching rain, looking up at the sun, low in the sky, he sits thinking it will be a hot day in the plains.

Ran makes his way through the hills, winding his way ever closer to the mountains. The low brown hills start to give way ravines and higher hills. Seeing an overhang farther up, he dismounts from his horse, walking up the small ravine. Feeling the weight of the last few weeks on his body, he feeds his horse, and then lays down for some rest. Ran wakes up later in the day as the sun beams down hard upon him. His horse is standing a few feet away. The sun is high into the sky. Yawning Ran stands up looking down into the plain he has come from.

Nothing can be seen moving on the plain, or in the hills below him. Studying the ravine that he climbed, he sees a small path leading up higher into the mountains, without a better idea of where to go he heads up the path, walking his horse. For a few hours he meanders up the path. Up ahead he sees a tunnel. Moving up to it, he can see light at the other end. Slowly walking through it, he sees the walls on either side of the path are now well over twenty feet tall. It seems to be made by hands as the ground is carved smooth. Drawing his sword, he mounts his horse, slowly moving up it. Throughout the rest of the day he travels along the path without seeming to make it higher into the mountains, until late in the afternoon he turns a corner with the world opening up in front of him. The plains are far below, in the far distance, he can see the Melcaren city, shining brightly. On the plains he can see movement of a massive army, towards the northeast. "The Melcarens must be heading to cut his people off from fleeing the devastation of Weldon, he thinks silently. Turning his back to the world, sees the shadows are quickly advancing on him. Moving up the path for a small distance he finds a wide place in the road, looking around he decides this would be a good place to stop for the night. He quickly unsaddles his horse, tying it off on a rock jutting out from the cliff wall. After feeding his mount, he lies down and is asleep in minutes as the night sky steals over the mountains.

Once again in the morning he finds himself slowly climbing up the mountain path. As he walks his horse he glances over at the cliff stopping. In the rock wall is a carving. A man's face is staring out at him from the rock wall, or what is left of it. The weather has eroded away most of it, leaving just the eyes and part of the top and left side. He seems to have a royal look, with proud eyes and high cheek bone. Looking farther up the path, he doesn't see anymore. Turning away from it, he continues on. The rest of the day is spent looking from one side of the path to the other. Ran doesn't see any more carvings in the rock, but the path continues on as before. He does notice it is getting cooler the farther up he goes.

The shadows have long since started to lengthen over the land. He notices the path has broadened out until it is easily thirty feet wide, and it has leveled out. He seems to have reached the top of a pass. He sees farther ahead that the road turns abruptly right. Spurring his horse on, he quickly closes the distance to the turn in the high mountain road, coming around the corner he stops dead still. Looking out over the end of the road he is stunned by the vision in front of him, fore a tall majestic castle juts out from a great flat open area. Thick marble walls rise hundreds of feet in the air. In each of the corners great white towers loom over the castle, a tall arched entrance stares back at him from across a precipice surrounding the castle. Reverently riding forward he see that everything is formed in smooth flowing lines. Nowhere can he see a hard line or divide in the rock. Even the battlements perched up on top of the castle walls are rounded into flowing lines. Spiraling out in to the air in the center of the castle is a huge tower far larger than the rest. Riding up to the bridge, he leans out looking down into the precipice. Being so deep he is unable to see the bottom, quickly backing up into the center of the bridge, he canters quickly across onto the field surrounding the castle proper.

The field is covered in the most brilliant green grass he has even seen. In awe he rides across the field, studying the castle in detail. Then out of the corner of his eye he sees movement, quickly turning it is gone. Thinking it must be a bird, he approaches the high arched entrance. Shadows hide any detail of the interior past the arch. Dismounting from the horse he walks slowly toward the entrance. The only sound he can hear is his horses' hooves on the white stone road. Pulling a stake from his bag, he sets his horse out on the grass.

Steeling himself, he enters the high arch of the castle. He enters a long forgotten realm. Looking around, he sees the room is easily forty feet long by fifty feet wide. On each wall hang tapestries' depicting kings and queens. Underneath each one is a suite of armor, looking as if it had been newly polished. Small white globes of light float in the air around the room, rich deep brown furniture is neatly placed around the room. In the distance it seems that he can just make out the sound of a harp. Almost a magical tinkling in the light air, walking farther into the room he sees a staircase leading through a door at the far end of the room. Slowly walking along the side of the room staring up at the tapestries he moves to the foot of the stairs.

Almost with regret he leaves the room, walking up the stairs intent on seeing the rest of the castle. Making his way to the top if the staircase he sees a grand hallway going to the right and left. Doors line the wall on the far side of the hallway. Rich dark reds curtain hang over the white walls, hanging in a line down the center of the hallway are the same small globes of light. Flowing like a river down the floor of the hallway is a red carpet in contrast to the white marble stone. Turning to the right he makes his way down the hall, seeing low benches nestled into the walls between the doors. Walking past the doors, he seems to be drawn to a small staircase he sees at the end of the hallway. Coming to the end of the hallway, he looks up the stair, seeing it disappear. Looking back, he starts up.

Up and up he walks, every so often he passes a small window looking out over the inner castle, he sees open yards of grass, and gardens, practice fields, walking paths among trees. He silently wonders how big this castle actually is. At the top of the stairs he comes to a hallway with three arched windows overlooking the southern plains. Far out in the distance he can see the inland sea, with ships crisscrossing it, to the southeast is the Melcaren capital. To the west he can see the plains dwindling into the distance. Closer to him, he sees the castle sitting on top of the highest point of the mountains. Pondering he whispers out loud, "Where am I?"

"You are in your city, Your Majesty." A voice says at the end of the hall. Spinning around surprised Ran sees a middle aged with brown hair and eyes, wearing silver and blue plate armor staring at him. Taken back, Ranquickly looks around, wondering how he came up on him without making a noise. "My lord I apologize, I did not wish to disturb you." Looking back at him Ran asks him, "Why are you calling me that, and who are you?"

With a slow smile, He motions for Ran to follow him, "My Lord, my name is Gaulin, and I have been watching the castle for ages waiting for the appointed time of your return. If you would follow me I think you shall find all your questions will be answered." Walking slowly, Ran follows Gaulin through the doorway and into a large circular chamber with high arched windows all around. In the center of the room is a simple low backed throne, unadorned or decorated.

"My Lord Ranwulf, it is the appointed time, for you to take your mantle on, you have found the lost castle of the Weldons. You have found Kimerion. The countries of this world are split asunder, each one battling the other. Our people have fled from the north. It is your time Lord. Sit in your throne and look upon the world."

Turning towards the small throne, Ran approaches it slowly. Reaching down, he feels the white marble stone cool to the touch; it seems to tug at his heart. He can feel through it the beating heart of the world. Sitting down, his vision seems to narrow, as he looks south, he thinks of the battle he fled out on the plains. Instantly, he is flying over the plains, looking down at the Delium and Melcarens in an all battle for their lives. Hundreds of Melcaren soldier litters the ground as the Delium are almost unstoppable. The hastily thrown up defenses quickly fall to the Delium force. Ranwulf can feel the blood soaking into the ground as the battle continues. Then after many hours, the Delium are slowly stopped by the sheer numbers of the Melcarens. The Delium force is forced back south towards the inland sea, without warning, they break free, riding swiftly southwards.

Looking back towards the west, Ran sees Antonius being pulled from under his horse; the Melcarens quickly bind his wounds taking him back to the city on the plains.

Looking eastward, Ran instantly is flying over a massive forest. Looking down from the heavens he sees grotesque shapes and forms skittering through the trees. Growls and screams assault his ears. Following the forest to the north, he spies a Weldon being brought down by a creature of the dark forest. Looking farther north, he sees the Weldons advancing farther into the forest. They are flooding the forest in massive number as the Turiec chase them. Panic mounts in his veins. He can hear the dying scrams of his people as they fight for their lives.

His vision passes farther north into the mountains, in horror he sees the Weldon cities in rubble, the Turiec have overwhelmed the Weldon nation. Countless of his people lay in the streets dead. As he passes west across the mountains he hears his name being called, looking out across the ocean to Britannia he sees a silver wolf speeding across the small plain hunting a Weldon woman. Speeding across the distance, as he comes closer he sees the woman is Feal, and impossibly the wolf is Balian. As he speeds past, the wolf slows, looking up at him. Turning the wolf makes its way back to the small castle to Mariale.

Ranwulf can feel eyes upon him as he turns back towards the north, far away in the castle he grew up in; he casts his eyes upon the northern wall. Travelling faster than thought he is looking down at Melcore, seeing him imprisoned in ice. He now knows Melcore isn't evil, just misguided.

Without warning Ranwulf is battered as he looks down upon his home. A figure approaches him from a distance floating upon the winds. As it grows closer he sees the figure is adorned in black armor engraved with runes. Holding his hand up, the figure is stopped from approaching any farther. "You are the one that fights my people." Ranwulf tells him. Meroth stares wickedly at Ranwulf, "You cannot stop us boy king, I have already defeated your people, and they are running into death as you wander the lands. You are too late." With a cruel laugh, Meroth silently disappears into the eastern mountains.

Turning back to Kimerion Ranwulf thinks of the room in the top-most tower, opening his eyes, he is back. "Gaulin, what has happened?"

Looking at Ranwulf, he responds, "Lord, the world is in turmoil, your people flee destruction from an old enemy. It is time for you to start on the journey to become the King you are destined to be." Gaulin walks to the window, staring out over the southern lands. "We have a long road to go down, Lord. The man you saw in the north is the true enemy. His attack on our people is just a pretense; his true goal is all the lands to the south. Our enemies lack the strength just as we do to defeat him. You are not ready for such a battle yet My Lord. The sword of the High Kings has not been found."

Chapter Fourteen
The Gathering

The rays of the morning sun slat down over the bogs, through a break in the clouds. Mariale and Balian look out over the marshland wishing they were somewhere else. "How did we get here Balian?" Mariale asks him. Searching for a way to get across to the town in the distance he answers her, "Don't know, just wish I could see a way across." They hear a rustle in the trees behind them, turning towards it, Balian grabs Mariales arm pulling her along the soggy path they have been travelling on. Each step in like walking in gooey grass, every time they pull their feet out a boot threatens to come off. "I can't stand this smell Balian; it smells like putrid rotting flesh." Searching the path in front of them Balian sees a drier patch a little ways away. Slowly mucking their way over to it, they stand on a small hill a little drier than the surrounding area.

A small tree grows out in the middle of the hill. Though looking more stunted than healthy. Watching a flock of great black birds in the distance, he sees one break away from the rest, heading in their direction. Searching with his eyes to the south he sees a small path leading from the hill they stand on. "That way Mariale, maybe we can make our way out on that." Balian tells her. Slowly walking along it, taking one tentative at a time, they make their way along it for several hours. Looking back north he sees the bird sitting on a small tree watching them. "I wonder what that is about, that bird has been following us for a couple hours?" he asks Mariale. Glancing back, she responds, "I don't know Balian; let's just get out of this then worry about other stuff later, ok."

Each time they look back the bird is closer to them as they near the end of the bogs. Finally stepping out of the marshland, they find their feet on firm ground of the open plains heading south. In the distance they can see smoke rising from a small walled town. They can see wagons entering and leaving it through a large gate in the north side. Guards stand relaxed near the gate, ignoring everyone.

"Well you two, you've made it farther than I would have given you credit for." Looking back they see a shimmering figure standing there. With a cry of happiness Mariale runs over to her friend, giving him a great hug. "Ran you're ok," With astonishment, she goes right through him, stumbling on the ground, she falls. Looking back in surprise, she sees Balian rush over. "Ran, what, I don't understand." Turning around to face his friends he smiles. "I'm not really here, I am at Kimerion. I want you too to join me there."

Looking at his friend he asks him, "Kimerion? Where's that? How are you here but not here Ran?" Mariale stands there rubbing her shoulder, staring at her friend. "Mariale, Balian my friends, I was taken by an Antonius a Melcaren commander. I was able to escape him after we were attacked on the southern plains." Looking at each other, they exchange looks. "What do you mean the southern plains, you're here on Britannia." Balian demands. With a sad smile Ran tells him, "No, Balian I'm not here in body, I'm here in spirit, I can't stay long, people are looking for me, and I'm not ready to be found yet. Head to the coast where we landed, Nellian and some of the nomads will be waiting for you." Looking at both of them, he smiles. "Along the way you should run into Feal." Quickly looking at Mariale, he grabs her by the shoulders in a hug. Looking at Ran he tells him, "Good, I can finish what she started, she almost killed Mariale, Ran." With a look of concern on his face Ran responds, "No, Balian don't hurt her, I know what she has done, she won't attack you when you meet her. I have talked to her, and need her to come with you." Shouting at RanMariale slams her fist on her thigh, "Ran, did you hear us, Derhuick, they tried to kill us!" Pulling away from BalianMariale walks up to Ran staring at his shimmering face, "Mariale, I know what they tried to do, she knows what I am going to tell you and understands what is needed, please just bring her along. She won't attack you, and knows to meet you tonight on the plains. I can't stay much longer; they are coming close to finding me here." Looking at each other, Balian is the first to speak, "What do you mean Ran, she know what?" With his eyes fixed on Mariale, Ran tells them. "My friends, Weldon is gone; an enemy from the north has invaded our cities. Our people flee to the southern forests trying to survive. We all have to bring our people together again if we are to survive." In shock, Balian and Mariale hold tightly on to each other, taking in the news of the destruction of their homeland.

Looking at them Ran tells them, "Go to the coast and bring Feal along, Nellian will deal with her once you get there."

"I have to go my friends, Hurry." They see the shimmering figure of their friend wink out of sight. Turning to Balian, Mariale asks him, "What do you think Balian?"

"Well, Let's atleast head to the coast and find Nellian," he answers her. "We can skirt the marsh and head over the plains. Turning their back on the town, the two friends start walking over the plains. Through the day they make their way along the plains towards the coast, near dark, they see a familiar figure walking across the plains towards them. As they get closer they see Feal, muddy, torn clothing holding onto staff to walk. When they get within twenty feet, she calls out to them. "That's close enough animal, I know what you are and don't want you any closer than that."

With a snarl, Balian starts toward her. Mariale grabs his arm reminding him, "Balian, No, remember what Ran said!" looking back at her, Balian nods. Shouting back at Feal with a snarl, "Ran is the only reason I don't finish what you started Feal!" Without a word, Feal turns away eastward, hobbling towards the coast. Keeping their distance, Mariale and Balian, start after her.

The waves crash upon the rocky shore, washing up the beach almost to her feet. Nellian looks out over the ocean catching sight of the small ship coming closer to shore. A small girl, she looks out of place in the desolate beaches on the eastern shore of Britannia. Holding a small staff, a small light begins to glow on the top of it. Nellian sees one of the sailors wave at her. Sailing into the small cove, they weigh anchor. Two of the sailors get into a small boat tied to the back of the ship, rowing to the beach towards her. Approaching the beach they row the boat to the beach, quickly jumping out and turning it back out into the water. Nellian hurries over, quickly climbing into the small craft. With expert ease, the sailors push it back out into the water, heading back to the ship. Once aboard, the captain, comes over to her welcoming her aboard, "Mistress, I am happy to see you once again, has it started finally?' He asks her. Hurit, yes it finally starting, we go to pick up Ranwulfs friends, and then we need to travel to the southern forests. From there we will go to Kimerion." with a bow he asks her, "which way Mistress?' Pointing south she responds, "There is a rocky beach, a few miles to the south, they will be there in a couple days. The captain shouts to the men, commanding them to pull anchor and set sail south. Nellian walks below deck to the cabin put aside for her, sitting down to think of the next few days.

Through the rest of the day Balian and Mariale, walk across the open plains, near evening they see a lone figure walking south towards them. As the sun sinks below the horizon, they see an overhang up ahead. Walking towards it, they see it goes a few feet under the rocky hill facing east. Feal is sitting down on the far end, rubbing her leg. Mariale and Balian look towards her. Seeing them she tells them, "I'm not walking any farther tonight, you can if you want, but I need to rest." Turning away she nestles up against the back wall, covering her face with her cloak, she turns away from them motionless. Looking at Mariale, Balian moves underneath the overhang, waving for Mariale to follow him. "It seems we have a small truce here with her, she is right about one thing, and we need to get some sleep Mariale." Walking to the back of the overhang, Mariale sits down with her back to the wall, glaring over at the motionless form of Feal. "Fine, Balian, but one of us needs to stay awake and watch her," sitting down next to her Balian answers, "I will stay awake for a while Mariale, get some sleep." Leaning against Balian, Mariale yawns a great big yawn, nestling against him, I am exhausted Balian, when you get tired, wake me up." Within a few minutes Mariale is sound asleep, leaving Balian to keep an eye onFeal.

As Balian sits there, looking out into the darkness the winds begin to start blowing. A cold and biting wind whips underneath the small overhang, bringing small drops of rain with it. Mariale scrunches closer to Balian. After some time his arm starts going numb from not moving it. He's caught, he can't move, but his arm is beginning to hurt now. When it starts to become unbearable, he decides to try to gently move Mariale, before he can move he feels eyes staring at him. Looking out, he can't see anyone, but sure as the stars rise in the night sky, he can feel someone or something staring at him. Farther down, he sees Feal moving around restlessly, then in a start she wakes up. Sitting up abruptly, she bumps her head on the overhang, grabbing the top of her head she curses softly. Looking over at Balian she motions out into the dark. Feal positions herself to jump up quickly.

Balian brings his finger to his lips motioning her to be quiet. Gently he reaches over shaking Mariale, he whispers in her ear, "Mariale, wake up." As Balian feels Mariale beginning to wake up he grabs her with his free arm, holding from moving, "Mariale, don't move," he tells her. Opening her eyes, with a look she silently asks him what is going on. Watching the darkness outside Balian sees a shadow deeper than the darkness move closer. Slightly moving Mariale, he feels with an intense amount of pain the feeling come back into his arm, he sits there slowly bends his fingers trying to make the pain go away. From the darkness the shadow gets deeper and bigger. Quickly, Balian jumps up, drawing his short sword in one swift movement, as Feal and Mariale move to either side of Balian. The shadow from outside slowly materializes into a tall man wearing jet black armor, holding a black sword with blue energies rippling along the blade.

What strikes their eyes are the golden eyes staring back at them from the man's face. He slowly walks toward them, stopping a small distance away. With a smile on his face, a small chuckle escapes his mouth. Standing next to Balian, Feal illuminates the ground around them with a light from her staff. Seeing nothing else she turns back to the figure. Looking at him closer she sees his armor is intricately engraved with magical runes. Staring at him, she breaks the silence, "who are you?"

Looking at the three, he turns his attention to Balian, "Tell your pathetic friend to shut up wolf, my words are for you." Feal starts to move towards the figure as Balian grabs her arm

"Stop Feal." Balian looks at the figure in black, "answer her question and how do you know me?" Looking intently at Balian, Meroth responds, "You don't need my name, nut I do know the spirit running in your veins, I wanted to see if it was true that the Werinrdrysd spirit is back in this world after so many ages gone, I believed I had killed your kind off ages ago."

Silently studying the figure Balian looks to Feal, understanding she knows more than she is letting on, "If that is all you can leave, I have no wish to talk to you." Balian tells him. With a high haunting laugh, Meroth slowly disappears into the night. Letting go of Feals' arm he turns on her, "Feal, you know this figure, tell me!" Silently Feal turns around slowly shaking her head; Balian prepares to grab her again, seeing Balian tense Mariale grabs him, stopping him. With a shake of her head, he stops looking at her. Stopping, Feal turns looking at them, "That creatures name is Meroth; he is the King of the Turiec."

In confusing Balian begins to ask a question, "What are you- "Feal holds up her hand motioning him to be quiet. "Balian, that creature is the one and the same that caused the destruction of our cities. The Turiec have invaded our nation. He is their King." Her shoulders bowing with despair, she sits heavily on the ground. Looking back up at them Feal continues, "I was sent to find Ranwulf and bring him back, that was the councils command, I now know we were misguided. Ranwulf is the only one that can face that monstrosity. I don't understand all that is going on, but we need to get to that ship so we can get back to the mainland. Our people are fleeing for their lives across the lands and we need to help them. The Turiec will not stop until we are all dead." Sitting down next to Feal, Balian looks at her with sorrow on his face, "tell me Feal, the Turiec—right? Who are they and why do they seek our destruction?"

"We can talk as we walk, we have to get going, you two." Feal says as she stands up. Following her, they walk out into the dark with the Feal leading the way with her light. After a few minutes Feal begin again, "Meroth was the king of the lands we live-or I should say lived in. When we settled in the north, we fought his people and overran their lands. They were banished to the northern wastes, while took over their cities. That's was hundreds of years ago though, Melcore was the only one alive during that time, what I am telling you is what I learned from scrolls and Melcore." Mariale looks over at Feal with a question, "Why did we take over their homes?"

"The history of our people tells of a time when we lived in the southern plain, but the Melcaren people invaded our nation, pushing us into the north. We had no choice but to flee north into the Turiec lands. After we invaded their lands the king disappeared, and left Melcore to lead us. I don't know why or what Melcore knows but Ranwulf is prophesied to become the High King. Prophesy regarding him say he will split the lands. But, if the lands are to survive this onslaught from the Turiec people we all will have band together. Even then I do not know if we can beat them. Ranwulf is destined to be the next high king over the lands, but he must survive." Looking at Feal sharply Balian demands of her, "What do you mean if he survives?"

Answering him, she says, "He won't come into his full power until he finds the high kings sword and brings all of the nations together. Unless he does that, we can't hope to survive. Meroth will stop at nothing to kill him. He is vulnerable until he takes up his mantle."

Walking next to her, Balian is silent for a few minutes, slowly thinking about what she told him. "Then why did you and Derhuick try to kill him?" Feal answers him, "We didn't try to kill him we were trying to bring him back to Weldon to be trained by the council."

"From what I saw you weren't training him, you were torturing him, you and your precious council!" snarls Balian. Looking at him Feal answers, "you think that was torture, wait to see what happens if Meroth captures him, and wait and see what happens to the world ancestor forbid if that happens." She snaps back. In the distance the sun begins to climb over the horizon. They can see the headlines of the coast. Quickening her step, Mariale and Balian hurry to follow her. Without speaking, they approach the cliffs. The staircase they walked up when they first arrived appears out of the morning light. Walking up to it, Balian and Mariale lead Feal into the doorway. Swiftly walking down the stairs, Balian and Mariale wait at the bottom for Feal to catch up. Scanning the ocean they can't see a boat, turning to the other two, Balian says, "Well, I guess we need to look north for the ship, we came ashore some distance in that direction."

They hear a quick intake of breath from Feal as they start out of the lower opening onto the beach. Stopping they look back at Feal; she is staring ahead of them at something. Turning Balian sees Nellian standing there smiling at them, with a shout of joy Mariale rushes over grabbing Nellian in a big hug. Hugging her back Nellian disengages herself from her facing Feal. "Yes, it is me Feal; it has been a long time since we met." Glaring at her Feal answers, "how are you involved in this, you were exiled long ago from our people!" Looking sadly at Feal Nellian answers her, "Feal I am-" glaring with hatred evident on her face Feal continues interrupting her, "If I had known you were involved I would have refused to come!"

Looking at them both Mariale speaks up, "Why do you two hate each other so much?" Without moving her eyes off Nellian

Feal responds coarsely, "This woman is not what she seems, she is a usurper and a traitor of our people." Mariale and Balian sharply look at Nellian, "That's a lie Feal, and you know it. The council was making decisions that would destroy our people. I tried to stop it and Melcore banished me." Walking toward her with the hatred growling from her voice Feal responds to her, "You tried to take the council from Melcore; we had no choice but to banish you, you would have torn the council and our people apart."

Looking at Balian and Mariale, Feal tells her, "Why don't you show your true form and not the pretense as a little girl Nellian?" Looking back at Nellian they see her image blur and shimmer in the morning light, in its place a beautiful young lady stands. "This doesn't change anything Feal, Ranwulf commands us to join him at Kimerion and you are coming along whether you want to or not. If you and the council would have listened to me, maybe we wouldn't be in the straits we are now, Feal."

Ignoring the last comment Feal shoots back venomously "Oh, trust me Nellian I am coming along, I will keep your dirty usurpers hands off him. Where is this ship he spoke of?" pointing to the north Nellian responds, "It is just up the coast, I wanted to see your reception of me before they approached." Within seconds two men appear, beckoning to them. Without a word Nellian turns around walking towards them, silently they all follow her. Walking around a corner in the cliff walls they see a small boat sitting on the beach. The two men are turning it, getting ready to put out in the waves. All of them climb aboard as they push off from the beach. Within seconds they are gliding away from the beach heading out into the ocean. From up the coast a ship appears as they move out from the coastline, heading in their direction.

Quickly coming alongside the ship they climb aboard the small ship. The captain walks u to Nellian asker "Mistress, are we ready to set sail for the mainland?" Looking at Feal, Nellian responds, "Yes captain, let's get moving." With a signal from their captain, the ship is quickly underway heading away from the coast. Pointing to the foredeck Nellian motions toward a cabin, you three can share that cabin, and we should be to the coast in a day or two." Without a word Nellian walks away to the main deck disappearing into the hull of the ship. With a snort, Feal turns away, heading to the foredeck. Feal slams the door after she enters the cabin, on deck Mariale and Balian silently followsFeal into the foredeck. Balian and Mariale walk into the cabin, Feal is already lying on a bunk turned towards the wall ignoring them. With a sarcastic tone Balian looks at Mariale, "Well, this is going to be a fun trip Mariale." Looking around the cabin they see a bunk on the far side, Mariale and Balian silently lay down, quickly falling asleep.

Shouts from the deck wake Balian from his slumber, Stretching Balian swings his legs off the bed, looking around the cabin. He sees Feal is gone. Again he hears shouts from the deck, "Lo Ho captain." Answering the shout the captain answers, "Which way sailor?" The sailor shouts back, "To the east captain!" Quickly waking up, Balian quietly makes his way onto the deck, opening the door he sees Feal and Nellian standing near the rail, looking at each other glaring. Swiftly moving the other direction he walks over to the rail looking out. In the distance he sees a forest coming into views as he hears a voice behind him. "Balian," a sweet soft voice calls him, "it's ok, don't worry you about our arguments." Recognizing Nellian, he turns to her, "What is going on, if I didn't know better, you two are ready to kill each other." Looking at him with sympathy, she responds, "As you know already she can be very, well to put it simply, a little extreme with things." Seeing a smile on her lips, Balian smiles back. "That I know Nellian, her and Derhuick tried to kill us out in the plains, the only reason, I don't do the same to her is Ran needs us all." Looking back over the water, he continues, "What do we do Nellian, how do we get along enough to see this thing through? You have a much longer history with her, how do you do it?" With a backwards glance at Feal, Nellian answers, "Well Balian, I just keep the fact in the front of my head that the fate of our world is riding on us all getting along and fighting our common enemy. As much as I don't like her rabid ways, she wants the same as we do, we just have to keep a tight rein on her. Keep an eye on her and we will deal with things if she decides to do something that hurts us. Other than that, I don't think we can do much."

Grabbing his hand, she squeezes it tightly, quietly turning and walking away. Looking after her for a moment, Balian turns back around looking out to the forest approaching. He feels familiar arms wrap around his chest, leaning back he squeezes them, standing there against the rail, feeling the wind blow through his hair.

Shortly before dark they make the coast, gliding into a hidden bay. With a hoop and a holler, Balian jumps into the boat as it is lowered into the water. Mariale follows him, as Nellian and Feal climb down. Looking back up, Nellian tells the captain, "Wait for us, we will be back captain." With a salute the captain orders the boat lowered into the water. After they cast off, they can hear the captain ordering his men to tie the ship down.

Balian grabs the oars, slowly rowing the boat towards the shore. As they reach the beach, Feal steps ashore followed by the others. As Balian steps out he is surprised to feel the small boat being pulled back towards the ship. Balian looks back to the captain, on deck he has his hands moving in an intricate pattern in the air as the boat floats back to the ship. Shaking his head, Balian turns back to the others seeing them head into the edge of the forest, silently he curses life.

Throughout the morning they make their way along a forest path, steadily heading east. Feal, following behind them with daggers coming from her eyes at Nellian, Balian and Mariale walk in the middle feeling like they are caught in a trap between two enemies. Up ahead, Nellian walks softly whistling to herself. In the distance, a large flock of birds erupt from the treetops. Stopping in midstride, Nellian motions for them to stop. Feal keeps walking until she is side by side with Nellian. "What's this about girl? More of your tricks" Without looking at Feal, Nellian backhands her in the mouth, Feal swings around at her ready to attack, but the look on her face stops her. Balian, rushes up to them, confused about what is going on. Nellian holds her finger to her lips commanding silence. From the forest ahead, they can hear gruff voices. "What are we doing here; we aint seen anyone in weeks." One of the voices says. Another voice echoes from the forest up ahead, "Just shut up fool and do what you're told!"

Nellian points to the forest to the right, motioning for them to follow here as she starts away through the brush. They creep along slowly moving away from the voices. Balian doesn't hear anyone ahead as the start up a long hill. At the top they see they have come back to the very same hill they were at weeks ago. The same tree is perched at the top as they crest it; wearily they all sit down, happy for a small break. Nellian points down the other side towards the east. "We will wait here for a bit." Looking at feal, Nellian give her a hard cold stony stare, "Feal the next time you don't do as you're told, when your told, I will kill you! You will not betray us with your stupidity. Do you understand woman?" Without speaking Feal coldly stares back, but simply nods at Nellian.

Mariale and Balian exchange glances, wondering who is who. Down the bottom of the hill they hear a strange call. Like a bird, but never like one they have heard before. Nellian looks down towards it, answering in the same strange call. As Nellian stands up, they see Weldons coming up the slope towards them. They are dressed in the brown and greens of the forest. Nellian waves to them as they come closer. "Welcome Neiron, I am glad to see you and your people." She says to the leader as he walks up to them. "Nellian, I'm glad to see you too, I hope it wasn't too hard to travel through the forest? We have been trying to clear a path for weeks now, since we got word from you." Smiling at him Nellian answers, "No, we had a close call with a couple Melcarens a little ways back, but we were able to sneak past." Neiron looks at her companions, stopping at Feal for a few moments. Turning to Nellian he asks her, "These are your friends your message told us about?"

"Yes, Neiron they are, we must get to Kimerion soon. Things are moving swiftly. Have you seen any Weldons travelling through the forest this way Neiron?" Nellian asks him. With a scornful glare at Feal he responds, "No Nellian, we haven't yet. When we do what should we do, we can't send them into the plains towards Kimerion. The Melcarens are massing on their borders waiting for our people to break through."

Looking to the east she answers him, "No Neiron, hide them as much as you can, when everything is ready we will come get them and your scouts." With a smile, he looks at her, "Are you ready for the journey east mistress Nellian?" He asks her. "Yes, we need to make a few miles deeper into the forest today before we rest." Without a word, Neiron turns around heading back down the hill into the forest, leaving them to follow him. With a backwards glance at them, she motions them to follow her.

Chapter Fifteen
Melcaren Revenge

After what seemed like hours Antonius is finally pulled out from underneath his mount. Almost passing out from the pain, he can tell that both his legs are broken. The soldiers quickly bind his legs, moving him onto a stretcher. The army has beaten off the attack of the Delium. Recalling the last moments of the battle before his horse was butchered, he remembers his Feriot striking at the Delium using magic. Berating himself for not seeing it sooner, he commands the soldiers to hurry. Swiftly moving to the army, they lay Antonius inside a tent, quickly leaving to fetch a healer. After a few moments a man in middle years comes into the tent, looking at Antonius he pulls the cover away from his legs. Without speaking he quickly cuts his pants away. Bones stick out of the skin in multiple places, oozing blood.

The man starts moving his hands over his legs in intricate gestures. Slowly, the blood stops flowing as Antonius screams out in pain. He can hear the bones moving and grinding back into place as the man continues his gestures. Unable to pass out from the magic flowing in his body, Antonius screams out again and again. Outside the tent soldiers cover their ears, moving away from the tent. In a matter of minutes, Antonius stops screaming as his bones are fuse back together, they last thing he remembers before he passes out is the man smiling at him, for inside his mouth Antonius sees he has had his tongue cut out.

Slowly, the man completes knitting the skin back together, only then does he leave the tent exhausted, mentally and physically. A soldier walks up to the man, guiding him away from the tent. They walk through the army until; they reach a section of tents in the center. A fence is erected around many tents, men, women, and children stare forlornly out through the fence. The man is led through the gate. Looking around, he smiles at a woman who takes him by the arm guiding him to their tent. Walking into it he lays down on a cot. Smiling at her before he falls asleep, she smiles back. A smile from a beautiful face he thinks. As she turns away he is reminded of their imprisonment as he sees her tongue is also cut out, their punishment from the Melcarens for being Weldon born, yet being forced to heal the injured and sick Melcarens.

Antonius sleeps through the night, in the morning he wakes to find a new uniform laid out on the table, with bath water waiting for him. Slowly getting up, he feels no pain, after yesterday. Looking down at his legs he sees they are covered in dried blood, quickly he takes a bath, dressing in his uniform. After eating a quick meal, he leaves the tent calling for the commanding officer. In minutes, a man in silver and red armor hurries over to him. "My Lord Antonius, it is good to see you up and about, I had thought it would be another day or two." Looking around at the army Antonius asks him, "How many men do you have here commander?" coming to attention, the commander answers stiffly. "As commanded we have emptied the city, we have twenty thousand gathered, ready to fight, My Lord."

"Very well commander, you shall take fifteen thousand of them and head north to the border, the Weldons are fleeing south as we speak. I shall take five thousand with me. Have them ready to depart in an hours' time." Antonius commands him. Saluting the commander walks away shouting commands to the officers. The army bursts into a flurry of activity as they quickly break camp, making ready to leave. A soldier walks up to Antonius saluting him. "Commander I am Mathura, captain of the western forces, I await your instructions."

"Captain, we will be going northwest from here, we track a boy. It is imperative that we find him. Are your soldiers ready?" With a nod Mathura responds, "Yes, Commander we are ready to depart."

Looking around at the men he snaps at Mathura, "Well, what are you waiting for, bring me a horse. Daylight is wasting." Jumping back Mathura orders a horse to be brought as he mounts his own. As soon as Antonius is mounted he they head northwest at a gallop, attempting to make up for lost time. Animals and people can feel the pounding of the hooves through the ground as five thousand Melcarens ride hard across the open ground. Out in front Antonius sees Ranwulfs footprints clearly on the ground. Only when they reach the hilly region of the plain does Antonius slow, seeing his footprint wandering among the low hills. Bring the army to a halt, he motions for Mathura to come over. "Captain, pick one hundred of your best men, quickly." Antonius dismounts from his horse, handing his reins to a soldier, he walks forward into the hills alone. Speaking softly to himself Antonius mutters, "What are you up to boy, I will find you and bring you back."

Hearing the captain walking up to him, he looks up. "Captain, are they ready?" Mathura responds, "Yes sir, hand-picked myself." Walking back to his horse, he looks over the men chosen, standing up in his stirrups he tells them, "Men, we will be searching for a boy, it is imperative that we find him and take him back to the great Priruit." Turning to the captain Antonius commands him, "Captain, take your men and moves north to the gap in the mountains, spread out between the feet of the mountains. Stop any that come through and hold them for me. Do you understand your orders?"

With a salute he responds, "Yes Commander,' Without another word he mounts his horse, commanding the army to follow him, in a few minutes Antonius and his small detachment are left behind waiting for the dust to clear. Looking around, Antonius sees a small set of prints heading into the hills. Looking around he tells the soldiers, "Keep your eyes open, this boy is tricky, as soon as you see something let me know." Without another word, Antonius slowly leads his column into the hills following the meandering tracks.

A few hours go by without any sign other than the footprints, and then coming up to a small overhang, Antonius sees signs of a small camp a couple days old. He can see the footprints scattered around the area in all directions. Looking on the northern side he sees they once again head that way into the mountains. Searching the terrain up ahead, Antonius sees the trail become rocky with many pitfalls and jagged rocks. He can see a small path wandering up the side of the mountainside. Picking out ten men he tells them, "Men you ten will stay here and keep care of the horses, the rest of you follow me. Leave anything that will slow you down, take just water and weapons. We travel fast."

Dismounting, Antonius hands his reins of his horse to a soldier, quickly dropping everything except his water skin and sword. Without looking back to see if they follow him, he heads up the small path following the footprints.

As the shadows begin to fall over the mountains, Antonius sees they won't catch up with the boy tonight, so he orders his men to find a comfortable place. "Men, find a place to bed down for the night, no talking or fires." Looking at the corporal closest to him, he tells him to organize guards for the night. "Tell the men, if they see anything to get me no matter what." With a salute the soldiers hurries off. Antonius looks around the area, seeing a place looking northward he sits down to wait out the night.

A shout wakes Antonius, instantly waking he sees a shimmering figure approaching from the north. The closer it comes, the clearer it gets. Antonius draws his sword, commanding his men to spread out in a line facing the figure. As it comes closer he can see it isn't Ran as he had hoped. Walking down the trail towards them is a man in a simple blue robe. He has brown hair, held back with a circlet of silver above his ears. Without speaking he fearlessly comes within a few feet of Antonius and his men.

Looking around at the soldiers he smiles at them. "You are trespassing on my land, leave now or face my wrath Melcaren soldiers." Walking forward a few feet, Antonius answers him, "We seek a young boy that fled in this direction, and we mean to find him at all costs."

With a small laugh, the man looks over at Antonius, "The boy is under my protection, you will not harm him commander. Turn and go back the way you came or face death."

Not being dismayed from the warnings, Antonius walks up to the man swinging his sword at his neck, without flinching the man stands still. Antonius is shocked when his sword goes right through the figure. Growling at him, Antonius yells, "I don't know what kind of magic this is, but head my warning Weldon. I will find the boy and drag him back to my leader, do not stand in my way!"

With a soft laugh, the soldiers see the figure slowly disappear into the darkness of the mountains. After a moment, Antonius turns back to his men. "Everyone, get some rest, for in the morning we start the hunt again." Moving back to his spot, Antonius lays down, quickly falling asleep.

Epilogue

Looking into the northern skies Ranwulf sees a storm gathering. A storm that will forever change the face of the world, it has already changed the face of the northern lands. Turning around he makes his way back into the castle. Looking around he sees al the empty chairs staring back at him. Soon he thinks they will be full. A long road to go down and no clear idea which way to turn while he's travelling it. All of his short life people have been forcing him to go different ways. Well, no more he thinks, if he is destined to be something, he will do it his way. He feels a different person than he was a short time ago.

Walking back up the stairs to the tower, he thinks on all the different people in his life. "Oh, what's the purpose, the only ones that didn't want something from him was Mariale and Balian. Possibly Nellian, but he would see about her." He mutters to no one in particular. Climbing the last few stairs he comes out onto the top floor of the tower, looking out he sees the expansive view on all sides. To the south he sees the Melcaren army slowly making its' way northeast to cut off his people. Looking west he sees his friends starting their way towards him. Turning to the east, he sees his people fleeing the destruction of their homeland. Hiding in the forest they are being hunted down by the wild creatures from the east. All he can think of is trying to help them, but right now he can't even help himself. He is stuck here at this moment waiting for the nomads to travel to him, waiting for his friends to get here. It grates on him. He feels a failure, but what kind of a failure he wonders. Everything was thrust upon him without his asking or wanting. Still, looking around he can't help but do what he needs to do.

He just feels like he should be doing more! Looking northward, he sees the Turiec army pouring through the mountains, destroying and killing everything that stands in their way. To them he is the bane to their people, because he is destined to be the High King. From his perch atop the mountain castle he can feel Meroth silently cursing his name and what he stands for.

Staring to the north he loses himself in thought, witnessing the destruction of the last Weldon stronghold in the north.

Meroth silently rages and curses the Weldon in his thirst for vengeance. One last city to take before he reclaims his people's homeland, Looking at the city wall, he promises that after this the Weldons will never dare to strike at him again. He sees a figure looking down at him from the battlement. A defiant people to the last, He had suffered loss in one battle so far, and he is not about to repeat that mistake. Meroth gathers the Solarus behind him, joining their strength with his. Blackness erupts from Meroth, inky dark nothingness emanates in waves from him. Looking down at him, the council member vows to strike before it is too late. Gathering his strength he waves his staff above his head, a yellow bolt of energy screams from his staff, striking the center of the blackness. It simply falls into it as if nothing was there.

Before the figure can strike again, Meroth brings his power to bear against him. Pointing his sword at him, blue energies crackle along the blade deafeningly. As the man on the castle begins to move away from the wall, he calls out in a strange language. A pure blue bolt of energy flies toward the figure. In an instant, he is incinerated. In satisfaction, Meroth calls him people to action. "Take this last Weldon City, let none escape, kill all you find!" he commands. Walking in front of his army, he leads them to the castle walls, from his sword blue energy blows holes through the gate. Without a word of command, the Turiec pour into the castle. Meroth can hear screams of pain floating back to him as he slowly walks into the remaining stronghold of his enemy.

Seeing a Weldon fleeing up a staircase, he incinerates him with a single flick of his sword, relishing in the fact of killing them. His voice booming over the castle, Meroth commands them, "Kill them all leave none alive!" moving from room to room, they destroy the castle and kill everyone they can find, Soon only the Turiec are left in the castle alive. Walking to the highest tower in the castle Meroth looks out to the south, smiling evilly he sees Ranwulf bowed with grief. "I have won boy king; your land is gone, your people fleeing to the four winds. You are powerless to stop me."

Bowing in despair at his people dying, Ranwulf falls to the floor overcome by grief. Slowly standing up with the weight of his people on his shoulders he vows to bring his people together. Looking to the north he shakes his fist at Meroth. "You will not destroy us Meroth; I will not rest until my people are safe and you are thrown down!"

Would you like to see your manuscript become a book?

Lightning Source UK Ltd.
Milton Keynes UK
UKOW050801300911

179551UK00001B/59/P